# In Search of Jesus the Christ

# In
# Search
# of
# Jesus the
# Christ

Harold M. Curtis Sr.

www.hispenpublishing.com

Douglasville, Georgia

This is a work of fiction. The characters, incidents, and dialogues are products of the author's imagination and are not to be construed as real. Any references to actual events, persons, living or dead, or to real locales are intended to give the novel a sense of reality.

In Search of Jesus the Christ

Published by His Pen Publishing, LLC

Douglasville, Georgia 30134

Copyright ©2018 by Harold M. Curtis Sr.

ISBN: 978-1-944643-10-2

Library of Congress Control Number: 2018934270

First Printing

Printed in the United States of America

This book is also available in digital eBook format

# Dedication

I dedicate this book to my descendants who I love very much. Most of all I dedicate this book to my wife Frances

# Acknowledgments

First and foremost, I would like to give thanks to the Creator of the Heavens and the earth for picking me out of all mankind to write this book. May it be a blessing to whomever reads it.

P.S. We all have done evil things in our lives that God has covered up so no one can see. So, when you hear or see someone doing evil pray to God to forgive them because we all know that the devil made Cain kill Abel and Adam eat from the tree of knowledge of good and evil. Both of them had direct contact with God. The devil cannot physically make us do anything, but mentally he will make us do things that we thought we would never do.

Don't let the devil deceive you, Keep God on your mind at all times.

# Introduction

Peace be upon you brothers and sisters. When I mention God in this story, I mean the creator of the heavens and earth. I would like to tell you a story about a man named Peter. I hope you will find it interesting. Oh, I didn't tell you my name. Everyone in the world knows my name. I think I will let you guess what it is. But enough about me for now. I'm anxious to share this story with you.

# Chapter 1

There was a Godly man by the name of who Peter lived in a small village near Syria. He was a righteous man that put his trust in God and God alone. It was a clear and sunny day and Peter was sitting by the window enjoying the warmth of the sun on his face. Children were outside his window playing. He enjoyed hearing children play. I could tell by the smile on his face. There was a knock at his door.

"Come in," said Peter as he opened the door.

"Peace and blessings be upon you, Peter. I just came by to see how you are doing today."

"Peace be unto you, Thomas. I feel real good today. I was just sitting here by the window listening to the children play, and thinking about Jesus."

"What about him?" asked Thomas.

"I have heard that he is going all around Galilee healing true believers of all kinds of sicknesses and diseases. If I could get to him, I believe he can restore my sight," Peter said.

Thomas laughed. "Are you drunk? No one can do such things."

"You are always doubting, Thomas. That's why no one can ever help you with anything," Peter replied.

"I don't believe it unless I can see it for myself. You know how people are, Peter. Like if you hit your toe against a rock and people see you, by the time the story reaches Galilee, it's been changed to a man lost his foot in a rockslide. You know people will change a story just to have something to talk about."

"I know some people change what they see and hear. But, for some reason, in my heart I believe the things I have heard about the man called Jesus are true. Some of the people who told me about him are righteous men. They also said that Jesus is preaching about the kingdom of God. So, Thomas I have a question for you."

"What is it?" responded Thomas.

"You can't see God, but you do believe that there *is* a God, right?"

With a sad look on his face, Thomas answered, "I truly don't know. I want to believe, but it's hard for me to believe in something I cannot see."

Another knock on the door interrupted their conversation. "Come in," Peter yelled without getting up.

"Greetings, brothers," the visitor said as he stepped inside.

"Greetings to you, Brother Paul," Peter replied, recognizing his friend's voice.

"Greetings, Paul," said Thomas.

"I just stopped by to see if you still wanted to go fishing today."

"Thank you for stopping by, but I cannot go now. Thomas and I were just talking about God and the man called Jesus."

"I've heard many good things about him," Paul replied.

"Like what?" asked Thomas.

"Someone said that Jesus' disciple, Matthew, told them he heard Jesus say, blessed are the poor in spirit; for theirs is the Kingdom of Heaven."

"I don't understand," Thomas said.

"Well, let me put it this way," Paul replied. "People who know they have a great spiritual need are happy because they know the Kingdom of Heaven belongs to them."

"I still don't fully understand," Thomas replied.

Paul smiled and said, "God, help me. I believe that Jesus was saying that people who have a great spiritual need are always praying to the one true God, and that makes God very happy. The believer believes that one of the things they must do to reach Heaven is pray to the one and only true God—the God of Abraham."

"Oh, okay. I understand now," Thomas replied. "What else did you hear?"

With a great big smile on his face, Paul said, "God is great. They also said that Jesus said blessed are the peacemakers, for they shall be called the children of God.

"I understand that," Thomas said.

Paul continued, "This is one of the most important things to me that Jesus ever said. Blessed are the pure in heart; for they shall see God."

"What does pure in heart mean?" Thomas questioned.

"I don't know what pure in heart means myself," Paul answered honestly. "Do you know, Peter?"

"Yes, I believe I do."

"Well what is it?" Thomas asked.

"I believe it means when you always have God on your mind," Peter answered.

Thomas looked at his friend confused. "What in the world does your mind have to do with your heart?"

"Let him finish, Thomas," Paul said.

"Thank you, Paul," Peter said. "When you are in love with someone or something, it's always on your mind. So that means if your mind is always on God, you must love

Him. If your mind is always on God, that will purify your heart.

"I do believe if a person could keep God on their mind all the time it would purify their heart. But, no person can do that," Thomas said.

"There goes doubting Thomas again," Paul replied.

Peter said, "It's possible for a true believer. A true believer tries to follow everything that the messenger of God did, or didn't do. Like how he takes his shoes off and how he puts them on. Like what he said before going into a place, and what he said coming out of the place. A true believer should know as much as he can about who he is following. So, if he tries to follow everything that the messenger of God did or didn't do, his mind will be on God all the time. Because, the only reason he's following this man is because he is the best role model for all mankind."

"Once again, you're right," Thomas agreed. "I thank God for putting you brothers in my life."

"We thank God also for putting you in our lives, Thomas," said Peter.

"You help us as much as we help you." Paul followed.

"But Paul, do you believe that Jesus has the power to heal all of the people that they said he has healed?" Thomas asked.

"Yes, I do," Paul answered. "Don't you, Thomas?"

Peter quickly said, "That's what we were talking about when you came in. Thomas said that he doesn't believe in anything that he can't see."

Paul replied with a surprised look on his face, "Thomas, I don't believe what I just heard. We are the children of Abraham. Surely you do believe in the unseen God?"

Thomas then said, "I fight with myself about this day

and night because I want to believe, but it's very hard for me to believe in anything I can't see. I pray that God will help me to believe in what I can't see." Thomas' eyes filled with tears.

Peter smiled and said, "Surely sight can sometimes be a curse. Look at me, I have no problem believing the unseen."

"You're blind," Thomas said.

"Yes, I am." Peter answered. "I can't see a thing, but I can see the truth. God has blessed me with four senses to bear witness to His truths. Truly Thomas, the truth shall set you free from all doubt."

Thomas cut Peter off before he could finish. "What are you talking about now? Four senses, and the truth shall set you free?"

Peter once again smiled and said, "God has said, in the name of God the Beneficent, the Merciful. I swear by time, surely man is lost, except those who believe and do good, and enjoin on one another truth, and enjoin on one another patience.

"What does that have to do with the unseen?" Thomas interrupted.

"Thomas, you need patience. You can't even wait for me to finish speaking. May I finish?"

"Yes, forgive me," Thomas said.

Peter continued. "I just told you what God said, and you Thomas asked my forgiveness because you know you have no patience. The unseen God knows everything we need before we know we need it. The unseen God has also said, that all true believers are brothers. Brothers should have patience with one another and help each other. May the unseen God help me to help you to believe in the unseen. The God of Abraham said we must believe in the unseen like

His angels, His Prophets, the Heavens, and the Hereafter. Let me tell you something else. Whoever says they don't believe in anything they can't see is lying to themselves and they don't even know it. That includes you."

"So, you're calling me a liar?" Thomas said.

"Please, let me finish, Thomas. If you don't understand when I finish then I will answer any questions you have."

"Forgive me again," Thomas said.

"Thank you, Thomas, and may the unseen God help me to bear to His truth. Do you know what the most important thing about believing in the unseen is?"

"No, tell me," said Thomas.

"The unseen God is what most people argue and fight about. The disbeliever will say I don't believe in any God that I can't see. But, when a true believer hears the disbelievers say that, they say there is a God you can't see. Then the disbelievers say to the believers, if there is a God that we can't see, prove it. The believer will reply, no one can prove that there is a God. That's where faith comes in. The disbeliever laughs and says, I knew you couldn't do it. But I say to you, a true believer can prove that the unseen does exist."

"You can prove that there is a God?" Thomas asked Peter.

"Yes," Peter replied. "And you should be able to prove it, too. You see, God has given most of us five senses to prove everything He says is true. Most of us use our senses for our own pleasure only. We must stop being so selfish. We have a responsibility to help our brothers get closer to God. We cannot help our brother if we have the evil one's hand over our eyes, mouth, and ears. Don't be like the three little monkeys. The evil one would have you to believe that the three little monkeys represent hear no evil, see no evil, and speak no evil. But, the true meaning is, hear no truth, see no truth, and speak no truth. I beg you to take the evil one's hands from your ears, mouth, and your eyes so that you may hear, see, and speak God's truth like believing in things unseen."

"God has so many things to prove His word is true. All five of our senses can bear witness that they believe in the unseen. Like on a very hot day, sometimes you can feel a cool breeze. You can't see it, but you can feel it. When you see a tree moving from side to side, you know trees don't move by themselves; it's the wind again. You can't see it, but you know it exists. When you hear shutters beating against the window, it's the wind again that you can't see. When your mother or wife is cooking and you're in the other room, you can't see the food, but boy, oh boy, can you smell it. The last is taste. When your mother tells you to close your eyes and open your mouth, you know there's apple pie, but you don't see it. These are your senses testifying that they believe in the unseen."

"You see, Thomas, everyone in the world believes in the wind, but no one can see it. That means everyone in the world believes in things they can't see. Right?" Peter was hoping he had proved his point to Thomas.

Thomas looked up with an amazing look on his face and said, "I have never thought about it that way before, or heard it put that way before. God is great. I thank God for helping you to help me." With a big smile on his face, Thomas declared, "I do believe in the unseen!"

"Yes," said Peter, "God is great. That's why I praise Him with my voice and my music. You see some of us have always believed in things we could not see. You know I can't see with my eyes because God has only blessed me with four of the five senses. I thank God for the four. He didn't have to give me any. Not being able to see can be a blessing."

When Thomas and Paul heard Peter's last statement Paul asked, "If not being able to see is a blessing, why are we going to Galilee?"

"Oh, I don't mean that I don't want to see. I do want my sight. But, most of all, I want to meet Jesus. I feel in my heart, when we reach him He will restore my sight with God's permission," Peter quickly replied.

With a smile on his face, Thomas said, "Well, Peter, if you believe we should meet Jesus then let's go to Galilee."

They all smiled and declared, "God is great!"

"You know Galilee is over two hundred miles away, and we have one big problem. We have no money," Paul said.

"If we save our money, we should be able to leave in a few months." Thomas said.

"Thomas you are becoming a positive person, and I like that," Peter replied, with a big smile on his face.

# Chapter 2

Months went by, then years, until it had been over two years since the men originally discussed going to Galilee. At last they had enough money to make the journey.

"God is so good," Paul said.

"Yes, He is," the others agreed.

Then Peter said, "I have so much to thank God for. He has always been so good to me. That's why I love Him."

"We should give thanks to God," Paul said, so they prayed.

"Can we leave now?" Thomas asked.

They gathered up their things to leave.

"Before we leave, we should map out the exact way to go," Paul said.

"I will make the map," Peter volunteered.

Paul and Thomas laughed.

Thomas said, laughing, "Do you want to write it yourself, or perhaps just tell us what to write?"

Peter smiled and said, "We should first stop at Byblos. From Byblos to Sidon is about fifty miles. From Sidon to Tyre is about twenty-five miles. Prolemais is about twenty miles from Tyre. We should travel next to the sea."

Thomas and Paul looked at each other and began to laugh. Peter started to laugh also. Thomas picked up a pencil and paper and said, "I'll make the map."

The three men headed to Galilee. They rode all day. It

was getting dark when Paul suggested they find somewhere to make camp and to eat.

"We covered a lot of miles today," Paul said.

"We could have covered more," Thomas insisted.

Paul looked at Peter. "There goes Thomas again."

"You're right, Paul. Forgive me," Thomas said.

Peter spoke up. "There is nothing to forgive you for, Thomas. It takes time to change and you are doing well."

The following morning, they got up before the sun rose and prayed, and then started toward the sea. When they reached the sea, Paul suggested they go fishing. The other's agreed.

"I love fishing," Paul said.

They fished for hours. Paul caught a lot of fish. Thomas wasn't catching many fish. He called out to Peter.

"Peter, how many fish have you caught?"

"None," Peter replied.

Paul then called out to Thomas. "How many have you caught?" he asked.

"One," Thomas replied.

With a big smile, Paul declared, "I have caught enough for all of us. Now who is going to clean them?"

"I'll clean them," Thomas volunteered. "But, someone will need to get the fire wood."

Peter spoke up, "I'll get the fire wood."

Paul and Thomas laughed.

"That's okay, Peter. I'll get the fire wood, too."

"I don't believe it," Paul said.

"I told you Thomas was changing," Peter said to Paul.

After Thomas gathered the wood, he started cooking. Peter told him how good the food smelled. Thomas thanked him for the compliment and admitted he hoped it would taste good. Peter assured him that it would.

When they finished their meal, Thomas turned to Peter and said, "You are mighty quiet, Peter. What are you thinking about?"

"I was just thinking about what it will be like meeting Jesus."

"I wonder what it would be like also," Paul admitted.

"I've heard that Jesus is like no one who ever walked the earth before," Peter said.

"I don't believe we will ever meet Jesus," Paul said.

Peter replied, "I don' know if we will ever meet him, but I do know one thing, if God wants us to find Jesus, we will. I think we should get some sleep now."

The others agreed and laid down on the hard, cold, ground.

Thomas raised up and looked at the other men and said, "I don't like sleeping on the ground."

Peter replied, "God willing, we will not have to sleep on the ground tomorrow night. I have an uncle that lives in Bybos."

"That sounds good," Thomas said. "Goodnight."

In the morning, they prayed, and then ate. After making sure they had gathered everything, they left and started on their way to Byblos.

"We should reach Byblos before dark," said Peter.

"I hope so," Thomas replied. "I don't want to sleep on the ground again tonight."

"Don't worry, Thomas. You will sleep in a bed tonight, God willing," Peter replied. "We know how many times God has given us what we asked Him for. We have so much to be thankful for. Maybe tonight we will be thankful for a bed."

13

Thomas smiled. "I hope so."

They continued traveling and talking about how many times God had blessed them. Before they knew it, they had arrived at Byblos.

Thomas turned to Paul and said, "Peter's uncle lives in this town."

"I know," Paul replied.

Thomas tapped Peter on the shoulder and said, "Let's look for your uncle's house."

Just then they saw an old man sitting down on a stump. They went over to the old man and said, "Peace be upon you."

The old man replied, "And peace be upon you my brothers. Welcome to Byblos."

Peter quickly spoke up. "My uncle lives here in Byblos. His name is Steve, son of Jonah. Do you know where his house is?"

"Yes, I know your uncle," the old man said. "He lives in the last house on the right."

They each thanked him.

"You brothers are most welcome. Enjoy Byblos." The old man said.

The three of them went to Peter's uncle's house and knocked on the door. The door opened and a tall narrow man greeted them.

"Peace be upon you, Peter." He gave Peter a hug and kissed him.

"Peace be upon you, Uncle Steve. These are my friends, Paul and Thomas."

Steve stepped aside and extended his arm to the gentlemen. "Welcome to my humble house. Come in, come in."

"Thank you," they replied and went into the house.

They were talking when a beautiful young woman came into the room. Steve turned to the woman and said, "Meet my other house guest. This is Ann."

"Peace be upon you, brothers," said Ann.

"Peace be upon you," they each replied.

"It's nice meeting you," Peter said.

"So, Peter, what brings you to Byblos?"

Peter answered, "We are going to Galilee to find the man called Jesus."

"I've met Jesus," Ann said.

"You have?" Peter remarked.

"Yes," Ann answered.

"Tell us about him. Where did you meet him?" Peter asked while Paul and Thomas stood nearby listening with curiosity.

"I come from a small town called Sychar, in Samaria. I met Jesus at a well in Sychar. He was sitting at the well and he asked me to draw some water from the well for him, and I did."

"Tell us more," Peter said.

"Jesus told me things about myself that he could not have known."

"Like what?" Peter asked.

Ann continued to tell them about Jesus., "He asked me if I was married. I said no. Then he said, you are right when you say you don't have a husband. You have had five husbands, but the man you are with now is not your husband, so you have told the truth. I told Jesus that I knew that he was a prophet. Then he said to me if I drink from this well, I will become thirsty again. But, if I drink the water He gives, I will never thirst again and I will have eternal life. I really

15

believe Jesus is sent to us from the unseen God."

Peter and the others could not say anything.

"Well," Steve said, "how long are you going to stay, Peter?"

"We are only staying the night," Peter answered.

"I haven't seen you in years and you're telling me you're only staying one night?"

"We are going to Galilee to find the man called Jesus," Peter replied.

Steve then said, "I know you are going to Galilee but you could stay more than one night, can't you?"

Peter answered, "I really would love to stay longer, but we must leave in the morning."

They talked for a few hours before Steve acknowledged that the men must be tired. When they all agreed that they were tired, Steve offered to show them where they would be sleeping. Peter thanked his uncle. He then thanked Ann for sharing her story about meeting Jesus with them. The men followed Steve to the bedroom he had prepared.

They started to get into the bed when Thomas stopped and said, "This bed is harder than the ground."

"You're always complaining," Paul said.

"Let him complain," Peter said. "One day he will stop when he realizes things could be worse."

"You're right, Peter," Paul agreed.

The next morning after they had prayed and eaten breakfast, Ann said, "I would like to go with you to help you find Jesus."

"We would be happy to have you come with us, Ann." Peter replied. "While we are traveling, you can tell us more about Jesus."

With a worried expression, Ann said to Peter, "I've told you all I know about Jesus. Do you still want me to go with you?"

"Of course, you can still go with us!" Peter exclaimed.

Moments later, Paul informed them that they needed to get going.

Suddenly, Thomas blurted out, "People might talk about three men and one woman traveling together."

"There he goes again, Peter," Paul said. "You see Ann, Thomas keeps us thanking God that we are not like him."

"I don't understand," Ann replied.

Paul answered, "Thomas always looks at the negative side of everything."

"I look at the positive side sometimes," Thomas replied. "Like when Peter wanted to leave home to find Jesus, I came along. That's looking at the positive side, isn't it?"

Paul smiled. "Yes, it is, Thomas."

"It's going to be a real good day," Thomas said.

Peter was not listening to them. He was thinking about the story an old man had shared with him about a man that came running up to Jesus and kneeled in front of him. The man asked Jesus what he could do to inherit eternal life. Jesus explained to the man that in order for him to inherit eternal life he had to obey God's commandments. When the man told him that he had obeyed all of God's commandments since he was a boy, Jesus looked at him with love in his eyes and said, "You're still missing one thing. You must sell everything you have and give all the money to the poor. Then you will have treasures in heaven." The man was rich and when he heard what Jesus told him to do, he became sad and went away. Jesus told his disciples "It's easier for a camel to go through the eye of a needle than for a rich person to enter the Kingdom of God."

"Peter, Peter!" Paul called out.

Peter turned toward Paul with tears running down his face and said, "Forgive me, I didn't hear what you said."

"Why are you crying?" Thomas asked.

"I was thinking about Jesus," Peter replied.

"What were you thinking about Jesus that made you cry?" Thomas asked.

Peter then said, "Sometimes when I think about God's prophets it makes me happy and sometimes it makes me sad. It makes me sad when I think about the things I have done that God told me not to do. I don't want to go to hell. I want to be with God when I die. It makes me happy when I hear what Jesus is telling the believers. Jesus is always saying that God will forgive us if we ask Him. It also makes me happy when I hear about Jesus always glorifying God. When any one comes to Jesus for help and is helped, they say thank you Jesus. Jesus says, 'Do not thank me, thank God. I can't do anything without God's permission!' All praise is due to the one God, the Beneficent, the Merciful. You see some things are impossible for man to do, but nothing is impossible for God, the Master of the Day of Judgment."

Paul went into deep thought and a strange look came over his face.

When Ann saw the look on Paul's face she said, "Peter I wish you could see the look on Paul's face."

Thomas asked, "What are you thinking about Paul?"

Paul replied, "Food."

They all laughed.

Ann suggested they stop so that she could prepare food for them. Peter agreed so they stopped, gave thanks to

God, and ate. Peter thanked Ann for cooking the meal and they started on their way again.

"I hope I can find a soft bed tonight," Thomas said.

"Don't worry, Thomas. We will find you a soft bed tonight," said Peter.

They had been traveling for many hours when Peter said to Thomas, "I don't think that you will be sleeping on a soft bed tonight, it will be dark in a few minutes."

"Peter, how do you know that it will be dark in a few minutes?" Ann asked.

"It's not hard," Peter said, smiling. "I can feel the sun setting on my face. Paul is there some place that we can make camp?"

Paul looked around and saw a big oak tree. "Look at that tree over there on that big hill. I think it will be a good place to make camp."

Thomas turned his head to the right and said, "Oh my God, it's the most beautiful thing I've ever seen in my life. Peter, I wish you could see this."

"See what?" Peter asked.

"The sun setting, it's so beautiful," Thomas said. "There are so many colors in the sky. It's breathtaking. God is great! To me a sunset is the most beautiful thing in God's creation. Sunsets are like God is painting in the sky. Everyday He paints another masterpiece for us to see. I wish you could see this Peter."

Peter looked so very sad. He said to Thomas, "Describe it to me please."

"I will do my best," Thomas replied. "You love music, right?"

"Yes," Peter answered.

"Well, imagine the most beautiful rhyme that you have

ever heard in your life. Then, multiply it by the largest number you know. That would not be a fraction of the beauty of a sunset. In other words, a sunset is God's rhyme in the sky. When we find Jesus maybe he will help you. Then you will be able to see the beauty of God's sunset."

Peter replied with conviction, "I don't believe when we find Jesus that he *may* be able to help me. I *know* He can help me, if it's God's will."

"You have very strong faith in the One God and His prophets. Like John the Baptist and the man called Jesus," Paul said.

"Yes, you're right. My faith in the God of Abraham is very strong and it gets stronger day by day," Peter replied.

Later that night, while they were sitting around the campfire, Peter asked the others a question. "Which one of these do you think is best to rule by—fear, respect, or love?"

Thomas quickly spoke up. "I believe it's better to rule by fear because it is said that Abraham feared God."

"How do you know that?" Ann asked.

Thomas answered, "Let me tell you one of the stories that my grandfather told me about Abraham. God said to Abraham, 'Take your only son, Isaac, and go to Moriah to sacrifice him as a burnt offering. Early the next morning Abraham saddled his donkey. He took two of his servants and his son. When he had cut the wood for the burnt offering, he set out for the place in the distance. Abraham told his servants, to stay with the donkey while he and Isaac continued the journey. "We'll worship and after that we will come back to you," Abraham told the servants. Then Abraham took the wood for the burnt offering and gave it to his son Isaac. Abraham carried the burning coals and the knife. The two of them started up the hill together. Isaac said to his father, "We have the burning coals and the wood, but where is the lamb for the burnt offering?" Abraham told Isaac, "God will provide a lamb for the burnt offering."

Abraham and Isaac continued up the hill. When they came to the place that God had told Abraham about, Abraham built the altar and arranged the wood on it. Then Abraham tied up his son Isaac, and laid him on top of the wood on the altar. Next Abraham picked up the knife and took it in his hand to sacrifice his son, but the Messenger of the Lord called to him from Heaven and said, "Abraham, do not lay a hand on the boy. Don't do anything to him. Now I know you fear God because you did not refuse to give God your only son."

"I don't understand," Ann said. "I thought God knew everything, so didn't God know that Abraham feared Him?"

"Yes, God *does* know everything. God knew that Abraham feared Him," Peter answered. "But God wanted to show the angels and the rest of mankind there was nothing that Abraham would not do for him."

"I understand now," Ann said.

Then Paul said, "I don't believe it. I agree with Thomas again. My father taught me a song that King David wrote. In the song David says, 'Fear your name.' David was talking about the name of God."

"I have never heard that song," Peter said.

"I will sing it for you if you want me to," Paul said.

"Yes, sing it," they all said.

*Listen to my cry for help, O God. Pay attention to my prayer. From the ends of the earth, I call to you when I begin to lose heart. Lead me to the rock that is high above me. You have been my refuge, a tower of strength against my enemy. I would like to be a guest in your tent forever and to take refuge under protection of your wings. O, God, you have heard my vows. You have given me the inheritance that belongs to those who fear your name. Add days upon days to the life of the king. May his years endure throughout every generation. May he sit enthroned in the presence of God forever. May mercy and truth protect him. Then I will make music to praise your name forever, as I keep my vows day after day.*

"That is a beautiful song," said Ann. The others agreed.

Then Peter said, "Even the Israelites feared God. My father told me a story also. He said the Israelites heard thunder and saw lightning coming from the mountain. They shook with fear and stood far away from the mountain. Then they said to Moses, "Speak to us yourself, and we will listen, but don't let God speak to us or we will die."

After Peter had told them that, he said, "Being afraid of God didn't keep the Israelites from sinning."

Yes, you are right," the others said.

Then Ann said, "You can rule by fear, but I believe that it is better to rule by love."

"Why do you say it is better to rule by love?" Peter asked.

"Because I believe that love is stronger than fear. For example, a woman would never fight a lion with her bare hands, because she would be afraid of being killed. But if a lion came and attacked her baby, she would not think twice about fighting the lion with her bare hands, because a mother loves her baby more than she fears death," Ann explained.

"You are right, Ann," said Peter. "I remember my grandfather telling me a story about Samson. Even as a child, Samson was very strong. He was stronger than his mother and father. His mother was not able to have children. God sent an angel to her. The angel told her, "You can't have any children, but I came here to tell you that you will have a son. Your son will be devoted to God from birth to death. He will be different than other men because he has a special purpose. He will become a judge and will free Israel from the Philistines." Everything that the angel told her came true. As strong as Samson was he always obeyed his father and mother. Not out of fear, but love. I do understand and agree with you, Ann but I also agree with Thomas and Paul."

"What do you mean you agree with all of us? Which one of us is right?" Thomas asked.

"All three of you are right. Most people think if they are right the other person must be wrong, but that's not true all the time. Thomas you talked about ruling by fear. And Paul, you also believe it's best to rule by fear. Now, Ann talked about ruling by love, but no one talked about ruling by respect."

Thomas started to say something, but before he could, Peter said, "Please, Thomas, let me finish. There is one thing we don't talk about."

Before Peter could say anything else, Thomas said, "What didn't we talk about?"

Peter and the others looked at Thomas and laughed. Then Peter said with a smile on his face, "Have patience, Thomas. I will tell you. Let me try to tie fear, love, and respect together with God's help. You might not agree with me, but I believe there are three stages in raising a child. The first stage is when they are a baby. The second stage is childhood, and the third stage is when they become a teenager. We all know that a baby does not know words. When a baby begins to crawl or walk, they will surely start pulling things down. Imagine a baby crawling over to a table and pulling itself up. The baby starts to pull everything down. What do you do? Well, some of us might run over and grab the baby and take the baby away from the table. Another way is when you see your baby pulling things from the table, you might shout, *no.* That might scare the baby. The baby may jump and turn around to you and cry. If that doesn't work, most of us will tap the baby on the hand and say, *no.* That is ruling your baby by fear."

"When a baby becomes a child and knows right from wrong then the parent can talk to the child. Sometimes just talking to them in a loving way when they do something bad will make them cry. That is an example of ruling by love. By the time the child becomes a teenager he or she should have a love and respect for the parents. But the most important thing is respect. Parents must spend a lot of time with their children. That is a must. Now let me tell you why children need respect for their parents. Sometimes a child's father or mother may die. The other parent may get remarried. The child might not love or fear the new parent, but the teenager should respect the new parent because that person is now their new parent. We should know that raising a child through fear alone will not work. If a child loves their parents but doesn't respect them, the parents will still have problems. But if a child respects their parents, they will always obey them. So now you see that you need fear, love, and respect working together to raise a good child. That means all three are right, Thomas."

"That's what I've heard that Jesus is teaching. That we are children of God, and God is our Heavenly Father,"

Thomas said.

"Yes, you are right, Thomas," said Peter. "You see the Pharisees and the Sadducees are only teaching us to fear God. That's why they are mad with John the Baptist and Jesus. Everyone knows that the fear of God didn't stop the Israelites from doing ungodly things. It's been said that God is all-seeing and all-knowing. A true believer must believe this. Believing this should help them not to sin against themselves or God. A true believer thinks of God being right there with them all the time. You know a true believer won't do a sinful act in front of their mother or father, so if God is with you all the time that means when you sin God is right there with you. Do you love respect or fear your earthly mother or father more than you do your heavenly father?"

Thomas said, "I remember someone telling me that the Sadducees and Pharisees came to Jesus one day. One of them, an expert in Moses' teaching, tested Jesus by asking him which commandment is the greatest in Moses' teaching. Jesus answered by saying Here, O Israel, the Lord our God is one. Love the Lord your God with all your heart, with all your soul, and with all your mind. This is the greatest and most important commandment. The second one is to love your neighbor as you love yourself. Out of all Moses' teaching, the other prophets depend on these two Commandments."

Then Ann said, "So that means Jesus is not the only one of God's prophets to teach that we should love God?"

Peter answered, "You are right, Ann. Even David wrote about loving God. David also wrote about honoring God. Honor and respect are the same.

"I have also heard that Jesus told the believers to stop

worrying," Thomas said.

"Stop worrying about what?" Ann asked.

"Jesus said, so I tell you to stop worrying about where you will live, eat, drink, or wear. Isn't life more than food in the body more than clothes? Look at the birds. They don't plant, harvest, or gather the harvest into barns, yet your heavenly father feeds them. Aren't you worth more than them? Can any of you add a single hour to your life by worrying? And why worry about clothes? Notice how the flowers grow in the field. They never work or spin yarn for clothes, but I say that not even Solomon in all his Majesty was dressed like one of these flowers. That's the way God clothes the grass in the field. Today it's alive, and tomorrow it's thrown in an incinerator. So how much more will he clothe you people who have so little faith. Don't ever worry and say, 'What are we going to eat, or what are we going to drink, or what are we going to wear?' Everyone is concerned about these things, and the heavenly father knows you need all of them. But first, be concerned about His kingdom and what has His approval. Then all of these things will be provided for you. So, don't ever worry about tomorrow. After all, tomorrow will worry about it itself. Each day has enough trouble of its own."

Then Peter said, "I truly believe that God will provide all my needs. I also believe when Jesus called God our heavenly father, Jesus meant that God will provide all our needs like a good father does his children."

"God is my father too, because He has always been there for me," Ann said.

# Chapter 3

"Let's talk about our first king—King Saul," Ann suggested as they continued their travels.

Peter replied, "The three of you may take Saul as your first king but I do not."

"I agree with Peter," Thomas said. "I learned from my grandfather that the leaders of Israel went to Samuel because they were angry with Samuel's sons. Samuel was old and he had made his son's judges over Israel, but they were dishonest. The leaders of Israel told Samuel that he was old. They wanted him to appoint a king to judge them so that the Israelites would be like all the other nations. But Samuel felt in his heart that it was wrong for them to request a king to judge over them so he prayed to God. God told Samuel, 'Samuel they have not rejected you, they have rejected me.'"

"Yes," Peter said, "You do understand Thomas. That day Israel did reject God because before that day God was their King. The creator of the heavens and the earth is still my Lord, King, and God. I will never call anyone or anything my lord, king, or god because these titles belong to the Creator of the heavens and the earth only!"

Peter continued, "What lord do you know that has more land than my Lord? My Lord is the proprietor of whatever is in the heavens and whatever is in the earth. And what king can match my King in being just, wise, and merciful? My

King is the most just, the most wise, and the most merciful. And what god can provide for his believers like my God? My God has brought food from the heavens to feed the Israelites. Do you know of any king that has more vicinity in battle than my King? Like the battle in Egypt between my King and the King of Egypt. Moses and Aaron said to Pharaoh, 'The God of the Hebrews has met with us. Please let us travel three days into the desert to offer sacrifices to the Lord our God.' Pharaoh refused to let them go and you know what happened. And what king can reward the leaders of his people like my King? Like Abraham, Moses, Joshua, Samuel, David, and Solomon. My King rewards his leaders in this life and in the hereafter. And what god have you heard of that has more power than my God? My god makes the sun rise in the east and set in the west."

Thomas said, "The creator of the heavens and the earth is Jesus' Lord, King, and God too. I believe this because I've been told when Jesus went into the desert the devil took Jesus to a very high mountain and showed him all the kingdoms in the world and their glory. The devil said to Jesus, 'I will give you all you see if you bow down and worship me.' Jesus said to him, 'Go away Satan. The scriptures say worship the Lord your God and serve only him.' Then the devil left and an angel came to take care of Jesus.

"You see Jesus called the creator of the heavens and the earth Lord and God and Jesus is teaching the people about the kingdom of God. Only a king can have a kingdom so that means the creator is Jesus' King also," Thomas said. "I thank God for letting me travel with you. I have learned so very much about the unseen God. I will never call anyone my Lord or my king again!"

"I know a story, too," Paul said. "It's about Daniel. Daniel was a man who truly believed in the unseen God of Abraham. Daniel had found favor with Nebuchadnezzar, who was the king of Babylon. I've jumped ahead of myself, let me start from the beginning. Nebuchadnezzar was the king of Babylon. He attacked Jerusalem. God handed the Israelites over to King Nebuchadnezzar. Nebuchadnezzar took the most intelligent of the Israelites to work in his house. They were quite knowledgeable in most subjects, and were to be taught how to read, write, and speak like the Babylonians. The king arranged for the Israelites serving in the house to be given the same food to eat. The Israelites were to be trained for three years, then they would serve the king. The Babylonian chief of staff gave the Israelites Babylonian names.

"Daniel had three friends named Shadrach, Meshach, and Abednego that were also Israelites. Daniel had made up his mind not to harm himself by eating the king's rich food or drinking the king's wine. So, Daniel asked the chief of staff for permission not to harm himself in this way. God softened the chief of staff's heart towards Daniel, but the Chief of Staff was afraid of them becoming sick or losing weight. He knew if that happened the king would have his head cut off. The Chief of Staff put a supervisor in charge of Daniel and his three friends. Daniel knew that the supervisor was afraid of the king too. He asked the supervisor to give them vegetables and water for ten days and then compare them to the other men who were eating the king's food and drinking his wine. The supervisor agreed because he knew that he could hide them from the king for months without a problem. After ten days passed, Daniel and his three friends looked healthier and stronger than the other young men who had been eating and drinking from the king's table. The supervisor never gave them food or wine from the king's table again."

Paul continued, "God gave Daniel and the three men knowledge, wisdom, and understanding of all the things they would ever need to know. God also blessed Daniel with the ability to understand visions and dreams. At the end of the three years of training, the king talked to all of the young men. The king only liked Daniel and his three friends so they served the king.

"King Nebuchadnezzar had a dream that troubled him very much. When he had more troubling dreams, he sent for his magicians, psychics, and astrologers, but none of them were able to tell the king what the dreams meant. Nebuchadnezzar became very angry with all of them. God revealed the secrets of the Nebuchadnezzar's dreams to Daniel in a vision during the night. Daniel told the king what he had dreamed, and what the dreams meant. Immediately after Daniel told the king, the king fell with his face to the ground and worshipped. 'Your God is truly the greatest of all Gods,' Nebuchadnezzar told Daniel. Then the king gave Daniel many wonderful gifts, and made him governor of the whole country of Babylon and the head of all the wise advisors in Babylon.

"Daniel asked the king for permission to let him appoint his three friends to attend to the affairs of the country, and to let them stay at the court with him. Nebuchadnezzar agreed. When the astrologers, mayors, magicians, and other heads of state heard that Nebuchadnezzar had appointed Daniel and his three friends over them, they were furious with Daniel and his three friends but not with the king. They plotted against Daniel and his three friends.

The king had a golden, 90-feet tall, statue made. When the statue was finished the king invited the whole kingdom to the celebration. The former head of state convinced Nebuchadnezzar to decree whoever would not bow down and worship the golden statue to immediately be thrown into a blazing furnace. The former heads of state knew that Daniel and his three friends were Jewish and would never bow down and worship anyone or anything other than the unseen God of Abraham, the Creator of the heavens and the earth.

"During the celebration, Daniel, Shadrach, Meshach, and Abednego did not bow down and worship the golden statue. Some astrologers came forward and brought charges against them and told Nebuchadnezzar about them refusing to obey Nebuchadnezzar's order. 'They did not honor your God or worship the statute that you set up,' the astrologers told the king. King Nebuchadnezzar became very angry. He summoned Daniel's friends to be brought to him immediately. He told them if they did not bow down and worship the golden statue, they would be thrown into a blazing furnace. Nebuchadnezzar said, 'If I order you to be thrown into a blazing furnace, what god can save you from my power then?' They answered the king, 'The God we serve is able to deliver us from the blazing furnace, if He chooses. And if He chooses not, we still will not honor your gods or worship your golden statue.'

"The king became furious and commanded that the furnace be heated seven times hotter than normal. Then the king commanded the strongest men in the army to tie them up and throw them into the blazing furnace. Shortly after they were thrown into the furnace King Nebuchadnezzar jumped to his feet and said, 'Didn't we throw three men into the fire? I see four men walking in the middle of the fire and they are unharmed. And the fourth man looks like the son of God.' Nebuchadnezzar went to the door of the blazing furnace and shouted, Shadrach, Meshach, and Abednego, come out! Servants of the Most High God come out here.' After they came out of the fire the king's men saw that the fire had not harmed their bodies and the hair on their heads wasn't burned and they did not smell of smoke. Then the king said, 'All praises is to your God. Your God sent his angel to save his servants who trusted him.'

"They disobeyed the king and risked their lives so that they would not have to honor or worship any other god except their own God. So, the king ordered that whoever said anything slanderous about the God of the Israelites would be torn limb from limb and their house turned into a pile of rubble. He promoted Shadrach, Meshach, and Abednego to higher positions in the province of Babylon."

# Chapter 4

Along their travels, many more stories were shared. Paul especially enjoyed repeating the stories his grandfather told him. As they sat around the camp resting, Paul told another story about Daniel.

I want to tell you another story about Daniel," Paul said. "But in this story King Nebuchadnezzar's grandson, King Belshazzar, is now the king."

"Okay, let's hear it," said Peter while Ann and Thomas nodded in agreement.

"King Belshazzar threw a banquet. Suddenly, during the banquet, the fingers of someone's hand appeared and began writing on the wall. The king became very frightened and sent for his psychics and fortunetellers. King Belshazzar told them, 'Whoever reads the writing and tells me it's meaning will receive a gold chain to wear on their neck. I will dress them in scarlet and make them the third-highest ruler in the kingdom.' But none of them were able to read the writing or tell the king its meaning. The king became more terrified. The queen said to her husband, 'Your majesty, don't let your thoughts frighten you. There's a man in your kingdom that can help. Your grandfather made him head of the magicians, psychics, astrologers, and the fortunetellers. His name is Daniel. He helped your grandfather to solve his dreams.'

"So, the king sent for Daniel. When Daniel came he told

the king to give the gifts and rewards to someone else. 'I will still read the writing for you and tell you its meaning. I helped your grandfather and I will help you also. So, with God's help Daniel told the king what the writing said and what it meant. King Belshazzar ordered that Daniel be dressed in scarlet and wear a gold chain on his neck. The king also made Daniel the third highest ruler in the kingdom. That made many of the people in the kingdom very angry with King Belshazzar of Babylon, and so he was killed that night.

"Darius was made king. King Darius thought it would be a good idea to appoint 120 men to rule throughout the kingdom. Over these men were three officials. Daniel was one of them. As time went by King Darius thought about putting Daniel in charge of the whole kingdom. Once again, the officials became jealous of Daniel. They tried to find anything Daniel was doing wrong in his job, but they could not find any fault in Daniel's work. The officials decided to see if they could find anything in his religious practices."

"What did they do?" Ann asked Paul.

"Well, they went to the king and convinced him to decree that for the next thirty days that whoever asked for anything from any god or person other than King Darius would be thrown into the lion's den. The king signed the decree and no one could change it or repeal it.

"Daniel prayed three times a day to the Creator of the heavens and earth. The officials knew this. They also knew that Daniel asked his God for everything."

"When Daniel learned that the documents had been signed by the king he went home to pray. There was an upper room in Daniel' house with a window that opened in the direction of Jerusalem. One of the times when Daniel was praying, a group of men saw and heard him pleading to God. They went to the king and told him what they had seen and heard.

"The king was very disappointed when he heard this. He tried everything he could think of to save Daniel from being thrown into the lion's den, but he could not because the law King Darius decreed could not be changed or repealed. So, King Darius gave the order to have Daniel thrown into the lion's den.

"That night, the king got up and quickly went to the lion's den where Daniel was. He called to Daniel with sorrow in his voice. 'Daniel, servant of the living God, was the God whom you always worship able to save you from the lions?' Daniel said to the king, 'Your Majesty may you live forever. My God sent His angels to the lions' mouths so that they could not hurt me. He did this because He considered me innocent. I have not committed any crime.'

"King Darius was overjoyed and he had Daniel taken out of the den. When Daniel was taken out of the lion's den the people saw that he was completely unharmed because he trusted his God. The king ordered that the men who had brought charges against Daniel be thrown into the lion's den with their families. What do you think about my story?" Paul asked.

Ann replied, "I didn't like the ending. Their families didn't do anything. Why did their wives and children have to be thrown into the lion's den, too?"

"I don't know," Paul said. "But I do know that the scriptures are made up of stories that tell us what to do and what not to do."

"You still didn't tell me why their wives and children had to be thrown into the lion's den," Ann said.

35

"The story shows me that a man can bring misfortune to his whole family," Peter replied.

"My father told me a story," Thomas said. "The sons of God saw that the daughters of the humans were beautiful, so they married any woman they chose. When the sons of God slept with the daughters of humans and had children, the children were giants. These children were famous long-ago. At that time giants were on the earth."

Ann said to Thomas, "What does your story have to do with Paul's story or with what I asked about the families of those officials?"

"Nothing," Thomas replied. "I was thinking about what Jesus said."

"Said about what?" Ann asked.

"If you hadn't stopped me from talking, I would have told you," Thomas said. "Jesus teaches that God is our heavenly father, so that would make all of us sons and daughters of God. My grandfather also told me a story. In the story it talked about the son of God. My grandfather said that God called Israel his firstborn son. Oh, I almost forgot. My grandfather also told me a story about King David. He said that King David said to the prophet, Nathan, 'I live in a house made of cedar while the Ark of God remains in a tent. I want to build a house for God's ark. But that night God told the prophet Nathan to tell King David that he would not build God's house but one of his descendants would. God also said, 'I will be his father and he will be my son.' These stories have been passed down from generation to generation."

"I didn't know that the son and sons of God were mentioned in the teaching of the tribes of Israel," Ann said.

Getting back to what we were talking about," Peter

said. "What God can do this? Like when Pharaoh and his army of chariots trapped the Israelites by the sea. Pharaoh and his army were on one side of the Israelites and the sea was on the other side. The Israelites were trapped between Pharaoh and the sea. The first thing the King of the Israelites did was send an angel to stand between Pharaoh and his people. The second thing the King of the Israelites did was open the sea for the Israelites to pass through. The Israelites went through the midst of the sea on dry ground. The third and final thing He did that day was close the sea on Pharaoh's army and they all drowned. Now, I say again what King can do that? And you tell me what King has ever saved his officers and soldiers from harm like the King of the Israelites. No one. Because only the King of the Israelites has power over all things. That's why the Creator of the heavens and the earth is my King. And wouldn't He be everyone's King if they only used common sense? Because no one wants to lose a battle, and everyone knows my King has never lost a battle and never will because my King is almighty, and all-knowing. When you fight in my King's army against His enemies you can never lose because my King is the only one who can reward you in this life and in the hereafter. And the last thing I will say is, my King is the most merciful."

"Our God is the Most Merciful," Thomas said. "I don't understand our ancestors. As many times as God has helped them, they still asked for another king."

"You know how most of you men are," Ann said.

"How are we, Ann?" Thomas asked.

"Most of you are never satisfied with anything once you get it. You always think it could be better. Most of you are not thankful for what you have. We all should be thanking

37

God, because things could always be worse."

"I feel the same way, Ann," Peter said. "I always thank God because I know things could always be worse. I can walk and talk and I thank God for having mercy on me."

"Look, there is Sidon," Paul said.

# Chapter 5

As they came closer to Sidon they heard music.

"They must be having a feast," Thomas said.

"It's not harvest time," Paul said. "I don't know of any feast this time of year."

As they came closer, Peter said, "It's not a feast, it's a wedding."

"How do you know it's a wedding?" Thomas asked.

"I can hear them singing," Peter replied.

"Yeah right," Thomas said. "Then tell me what they are singing, if you can hear them."

"You mean right now?" Peter asked.

"Yes, right now," Thomas said.

So, Peter began singing, *"Draw me, we will run after thee. The king hath brought me into his chambers. We will be glad and rejoice in thee, we will remember thy love more than wine. The upright love thee. I'm black, but comely. O ye daughters of Jerusalem, as the tents of Kedar, as the curtains of Solomon. Look not upon me, because I'm black, because the sun hath looked upon me. My mother's children were angry with me. They made me the keeper of the vineyards."* Peter ended the song. "See, I told you that I could hear them singing."

Thomas then said, "I know that song. It's one of the songs that Solomon wrote. I think it's the most beautiful song that he ever wrote. Well Ann, Solomon said in his song that he was black. And Solomon was David's son, and they also call Jesus the son of David. So, Ann, is Jesus black?"

Peter then said, "That's not the groom's part. It's the bride's part."

"No, it isn't," Thomas said. "That's Solomon singing to the young women of Jerusalem.

"I don't know who's right, but I do know that we can't go into Sidon debating about this," Peter said.

"You're right," Thomas agreed.

As they went into Sidon, Paul remarked, "Sidon is so beautiful."

Peter asked them to describe it to him. Thomas began to describe Sidon to Peter. "It looks like the whole town is covered in the most beautiful flowers I have ever seen. Everyone is dressed in the finest clothes. It looks like the whole village is at the celebration."

Just then an old man came up to them and said, "Peace be upon you all. My name is Harold, son of Joseph. Welcome to Sidon. Are you brothers and sister staying overnight or just passing through?"

Paul replied, "We would love to stay here overnight, if we could find somewhere to stay."

"No problem. You may stay at my house. I have plenty of room in my home for all of you."

"Thank you very much, but we don't want to be any trouble."

"No trouble at all," Harold replied. "It would make me very happy to have you as house guests. Come, enjoy the celebration, and make yourselves at home. Bring my guests some food," Harold ordered.

"Thank you," Paul said.

Harold replied, "Don't thank me, all thanks is due to God. The God of Abraham has blessed me with more than enough to share."

By that time the women of the village were bringing the food to them.

"Eat now and enjoy yourselves," Harold said. "I will come back to get you later."

One of the women who brought them food asked if there was anything else she could get for them.

"No, thank you. We have everything we need," Thomas answered. "Who's getting married?"

The young woman replied, "It's my sister, Burstelle's wedding. She's the oldest of the daughters. She's marrying Vincent, son of Eric. My name is Paulette and these are my other sisters Donna, Patricia, Lisa, and Vienna," she said, pointing to the young ladies standing next to her.

"Do you have any brothers?" Thomas asked.

"Yes," Paulette said. "I have six brothers. There's one over there, wearing white with a green belt. His name is Jeremiah."

"You have a big family," Thomas said.

"Yes, my father loves children," Paulette replied.

"What is your father's name?" Thomas asked.

"Oh, I thought you knew," Paulette replied. "Brother Harold is my father. You should eat before your food gets cold. I hope you will enjoy your food."

"Thank you very much. I know we will," said Peter.

They sat down and began to eat. Thomas took a few bites and said to the others, "We are truly blessed. This food is delicious and we have somewhere to sleep tonight. Maybe in a soft bed."

Ann smiled and said, "What are you trying to say, that my cooking isn't a blessing?"

"No, I didn't mean that," Thomas quickly answered.

Ann and the others began to laugh. Ann was still smiling when she said, "The food *is* delicious, Thomas." They all continued to laugh.

"Harold has some pretty daughters," Paul said.

"Yes, they are," Thomas smiled and agreed.

"There you men go again," Ann said.

"No, we didn't mean it like that," Paul replied.

Ann smiled and said, "I hope not. Remember, their brother, Jeremiah, is a big man and there are five more of them."

"They wouldn't hit a blind man, would they?" Peter asked.

They all laughed.

"You're something else, Peter," Ann said.

"I know," Peter replied.

A few hours later, Harold came back and asked, "Are you young men tired yet? They answered him, 'Yes."

"Women get tired too," Ann interjected.

"Oh precious," Harold said. "You're the one I came back for. These young men can find their way to my house by themselves. I came specially to escort you to my home."

Ann once again smiled and said, "Thank you. You are so sweet."

"I will see you brothers later," Ann said.

"And don't worry about her," Harold said. "I will protect her with my life."

"They make a nice couple, don't they?" Thomas said. He looked at Paul and they both began to laugh.

"What's so funny?" Peter asked. "If God wants them together, they will be together."

"You're right," Paul agreed.

"He does have a kind heart," Thomas said. "What are we

talking about anyway? What I said was meant to be a joke. Come on, let's go."

"Where are we going?" Paul asked. "Harold didn't tell us where he lives."

They went up to one of the men at the celebration and Paul asked, "Do you know where Brother Harold lives?"

"Yes brother, I know where Harold lives," the man replied. "Do you see that street over there to your left? Take it and you will see a big brown house. That will be Harold's house."

They thanked the man and departed.

They walked to the end of the street and looked to the left like they were told

"That's one big house," Thomas said. They went up to the door and knocked.

The door opened and Harold greeted them and invited them inside.

"This is the largest room that I have ever seen," Thomas said as Ann appeared and stood next to Harold.

"Yes, it is somewhat of a large room," Harold replied. "When I had it built I didn't want any walls."

"I can't see, but I hope this house has a second floor with walls," Peter said.

Harold smiled and said, "Yes, there's a second floor with bedrooms, but my room has the only door upstairs."

"I promise I won't peep into your daughter's room," Peter said, laughing.

Harold and the others started laughing, too. "All of the other rooms have curtains at the entrance. I know you all must be tired. One of my daughters will show you to your room.

They all thanked him. Harold replied by saying, "I thank

God for giving me enough to share with you. I will see you in the morning, if God wills. Goodnight."

"Goodnight," they replied.

Thomas noticed Ann wasn't following them. "Are you going to bed?" he asked her.

"No, not right now. I want to talk with Harold a little longer. Goodnight," Ann replied.

"Come, I will take you brothers to your room," Donna said. "I hope you will be comfortable."

They followed her to the room and offered her thanks. Thomas asked Donna where Ann's room was.

Donna answered, "You are on the side of the house with my brothers. My sisters and me stay on the other side of the house close to our father. His room is at the top of the stairs. Ann's room is right next to his. Our father is our protector. That is why his room is at the top of the stairs. My father sleeps very light.

"Donna, we have not met your mother," Peter said.

"Our mother passed away a few years ago," Donna replied.

"Hearing that saddens my heart," Peter said.

"Thank you, but it's okay. I hope and pray that my mother is with God. My mother was a true believer. She tried so very hard to be the best that she could be in God's sight. You would have liked her. Everyone who knew her did. Goodnight."

"Goodnight," they replied.

"Wow. She sure is pretty," Thomas said.

"I don't know what she looks like," Peter said, "but she has a beautiful voice. It's so soft and submissive. I would guess she is about five feet and around one hundred pounds."

44

"How do you do that?" Thomas asked with a puzzled look on his face.

Peter smiled and laughed. They each said good night and went to sleep. Several hours passed as they slept. An hour before dawn they heard a loud knock and a male voice.

*Knock, knock.* "Peace be upon you," Jeremiah said.

"Peace be upon you," Peter replied.

Jeremiah said. "Everyone is getting ready for prayer. It will be daybreak shortly."

"We will be right down," Peter replied.

They all met for prayer. After praying, all the men sat at the table. It was a few minutes before dawn. Peter smelled the aroma of food and asked, "What are they cooking. It sure smells good."

"It should. They get plenty of practice," Harold said. "The whole house must eat breakfast and supper together. That includes my guests also. How long will you be staying?"

"I don't know," Peter answered.

Another of Harold's sons introduced himself. "My name is Eric," he said. "What business brings you to Sidon?"

"Eric, it's not polite to pry into our guests' business," Harold admonished. "You must forgive my son, Eric. He's the youngest, and he still has much to learn."

"It's okay," Peter said. "What brought us to Sidon is no secret. Maybe Eric can help us. Eric, we are looking for the man called Jesus. What can you tell us about him?"

"Nothing really," said Eric.

"Harold, what can you tell us about Jesus?" Ann asked.

"You must go to my daughter, Nikki's house. She knows more about Jesus than I do. I will get my youngest daughter, Joi, to take you there."

# Chapter 6

While they were walking to Nikki's house, Joi said, "Nikki has been to Zarephath and Tyre to hear Jesus preach. Nikki loves to travel to different places. Now that she's married maybe she will stop moving around so much."

Then Peter said, "Yes, marriage does stop women from traveling so much and men. If Ann was married she wouldn't be traveling with us."

"Oh, she's not married?" Joi asked.

"No, what difference does that make?" Peter asked.

Joi answered, "Ann is with my father and you don't know my father. He's been married many times. If I know my father, he's looking at Ann as a potential wife."

"I hope not," Thomas said, sounding and looking worried.

"You should not worry," Joi said. "My father knows how to treat women. As a matter of fact, he treats women very good. That's why eight women have married him. A woman would be blessed to have my father for a husband."

"I believe when you get married it should be forever," Thomas said.

Joi replied, "Yes, you are right, my father told us marriage should last forever. But, we must accept that God gives and takes away. My father told us every time he married he thought it would last forever. He says that in the scriptures, God says it is not good for a man to be alone so he made

46

woman as a helpmate. My father says that the only thing that God says that man needs here on earth is a woman. Not money, not land, only a helpmate. My father also says a man can have all the riches his heart can desire and still be unhappy. But, the poorest man that has the woman that he wants to be with and she wants to be with him, that man is happy. That man would not trade places with anyone, not even for a mountain of gold. My father says he thanks God for sending Jesus to show him his mistakes. Jesus said, 'Listen, Israel, the Lord our God is the only Lord. So, love the Lord God with all your heart, with all your soul and all your mind. Moses told us the same thing but we seem to have forgotten. God is the most merciful to man, so God sent Jesus to tell us again."

"I don't understand," Thomas said. "What does that have to do with your father and his wives?"

Joi replied, "It's like this; my father fell in love with each of his wives but now he realizes that he should only love God. For example, if a man gives all of his gold to his wife he cannot give his son any gold, can he? My father said he loves God and God alone. My father also says if God blesses him with another wife he will treat her like a gift from God always. And you know when someone you love gives you a gift you take good care of it. It becomes the most important thing on earth to you."

Thomas then said, "I never looked at love that way before."

"My father looks at things differently today than he did a few months ago." Joi replied. "Here is Nikki's house." She walked up to the door and knocked. When her sister answered the door, Joi told her she had friends with her.

The door opened and there stood the most beautiful

woman Thomas had ever seen in his life. Her eyes were as innocent as a baby's. She had a smile that could light up any room.

"Peace be upon you," Nikki said.

Her voice alone would melt any man's heart. She was as dark as a moonless night with skin like velvet, and she had all the features that any man could want in a wife.

Thomas and Paul could not speak, but Peter could. "Peace be upon you," he said.

"I have brought these three brothers because they want to know about Jesus. Father said you know the most about Jesus so he told me to bring them to you."

"My husband is not home, so I can't invite them in," Nikki said. "But I will go back with you to my father's house."

"Okay," Joi said. "They are staying at father's house as his guest.

Nikki replied, "Oh good, then I will meet you there in about an hour. Okay?"

"So, we will meet you at father's house. Peace be upon you," said Joi and they turned to leave.

Paul said, "You and your sisters are pretty."

"Thank you," Joi said. "We take after our mother. She was beautiful. You would have liked her."

"If you are like your mother, I know I would have liked her, "Paul replied.

"What a sweet thing to say," Joi said.

"Do you think your sister is really coming?" Peter asked.

"If Nikki says she is coming, she will come. Nikki always keeps her word."

They had just reached Harold's house when Thomas said, "Something must be wrong. The door is wide open."

Joi smiled and said, "No, nothing is wrong. Everyone

must be gone, except my father and Ann. That's why the door is open."

"Why do you say that?" Thomas asked.

Joi answered, "The men in this village look out for the woman's honor. My father left the door open so no one could say or think anything bad about Ann. Our custom is when a man and woman are unmarried and alone in a house, they should leave the door open. That is saying to everyone we are not doing anything that you shouldn't see."

"Father, we're back," Joi greeted.

"That didn't take long," Harold replied.

"It didn't take long because Nikki was home alone and couldn't let the brothers in."

"I understand," Harold said.

"But she will be here shortly."

"Good," said Harold. "Me and Ann were just sitting here talking about how good God has been to us. I was telling her how God delivered me from a drinking problem. I like telling that story."

Thomas than said, "I would like to hear the story too, if it's okay."

Harold answered, "No problem. Please, sit down, all of you. I will start from the beginning. When I started school they taught me about God. My grandmother was the first one I saw pray to the One God. She made sure me and my brothers knew how to pray. From the age of seven I started to learn about the Word of God. I left home at the age of eighteen and moved to a smaller village. That is where I met the mother of my children. I still love her, and always will, I guess. She was the best wife and mother I have ever known. We were married for fourteen years. We had a lot of good years and some bad years too. When I left my family, it almost destroyed me. You see, from a child, I felt unloved. When I married and children started coming into my life, I was so very happy. I said to myself, my children will always love me no matter what. For the first time in my life I truly felt love. I was so happy God had blessed me with a family of my own."

"I made many mistakes in my marriage, but not on purpose. My marriage was falling apart. My wife and I tried to save it, but we couldn't. When I left my family, I became lonely and depressed. For the first time in my life, I began to drink to stop the pain of leaving my wife and children. But, it only made things worse. Drinking became my biggest problem. My drinking was taking me totally out of my children's lives. You see I knew drinking was destroying me. I had become possessed by the genie in the bottle, and I couldn't stop. I went to many places for help, but no one could help me."

"There was a man that I had been watching for about two months. I would see him about two or three times a week. He would be praying for people. He never took any money. One day he was telling a man that it's never too late to turn your life over to God. I was standing behind him, listening. Suddenly, he turned around to me and said, 'The Lord told me to pray for you.'

"We went to a quiet place, and there I turned my life over to God. In a blink of an eye, God freed me from my drinking problem and every other unclean spirit that had a hold of me. It was a miracle. So now when I tell people, I don't believe that there is a God, they look at me so strange. They can't believe what they are hearing. I know when people hear me say that they will not understand.

Do you understand, Thomas?"

"No, I don't understand either," Thomas said. "God helped you and then you stopped believing in Him."

Then Harold said, "What about you other two young men, do you understand?"

"No, we don't understand either," said Paul and Peter.

Harold smiled and said, "When God worked that miracle in my life, I no longer believed that there is a God, I *knew* that there is a God. You see, when you know something, no one can change your mind. But, when you believe something, someone may be able to change your mind."

"Peace be upon you."

Joi turned around and said, "Oh it's you, Nikki."

The others greeted her.

"How are you today, father?" Nikki asked.

"I feel very good today, thank God," Harold said. "These are my guests, Peter, Paul, Thomas, and this is my most beautiful guest, Ann.

"Yes, I've met everyone, except Ann," Nikki said.

"Peace be upon you. Your father told us you could tell us about Jesus," Ann said.

"I will tell you what I know about the man called Jesus," Nikki answered and sat down at the table with them.

"Thank you," Peter said.

"When I went to Tyre, I saw Jesus. He is truly a man of God. Let me tell you a story. A Canaanite woman came to Jesus and cried out, 'Have mercy on me son of David for my daughter is tormented by a demon.' But Jesus did not answer her. Then Jesus' disciples came to him and begged him to tell the woman to go away because she was following them and shouting. But Jesus answered the woman saying, 'God sent me only to the lost sheep of the nation of Israel.' The woman came up to Jesus and bowed down and said, 'Help me.' Jesus replied, 'It is not right to take the children's bread and give it to the dogs.' With tears running down her cheek she said to Jesus, 'You are right, but even the dog eats scraps that fall from their master's table.' Jesus replied, 'Woman you have strong faith! What you wanted will be done for you.' At that moment her daughter was cured."

Peter then said, "It seems like whatever Jesus asks God to do for him, God does it."

"You're right, Peter. God hears Jesus' prayers. Let me tell you what else happened in Tyre. Jesus fed many people with God's help."

Peter looked confused. He said, "What do you mean when you say with God's help?"

Nikki replied, "Jesus and his disciples only had seven loaves of bread and a few small fish. Jesus took the seven loaves of bread and the fish and held them up to the heavens and prayed to God, then Jesus thanked God for the bread and fish. Jesus broke the bread up and gave the bread and fish to his disciples. They gave the bread and fish to thousands of people. The people ate as much as they wanted and it never ran out. When his disciples picked up the leftover pieces of food they filled up seven large baskets. I saw these things with my own eyes. Jesus is like no other man that has walked this earth."

"I agree with you, Nikki," Peter said.

"My grandfather told me many stories about servants of God, but none like this," Thomas said.

"How long ago was Jesus there?" Peter asked Nikki.

"That was a few years ago."

"Do you know where Jesus is now?"

"No, I don't," Nikki answered. "Maybe you can ask Elder David. He is a merchant and he's always traveling. He might know Jesus' whereabouts."

"Where can we find this Elder David?" Peter asked.

"I can take you to him," Nikki replied.

"Thank you. Can we leave now?" Peter asked.

"Yes," Nikki answered.

They arrived at Elder David's home and Nikki went to the door and knocked. The door opened and Elder David greeted them.

They went inside and Nikki explained the reason for their visit. "We need information about the man called Jesus."

"I don't know much about him," Elder David said.

"Have you heard anything that could help my father's guest find him?" Nikki asked.

"The last thing I heard, he was at the Jordan River," Elder David replied.

"Thank you very much, Elder David," Peter said.

They left and headed back to Harold's house. Peter then said to the others, "Do you think we will ever find Jesus?"

Paul replied, "If God wants us to find Jesus, we will."

Peter answered, "You are right, Paul."

Before they knew it, they were back at Harold's house. They walked in and Ann and Harold were still talking.

Paul said to Harold, "Thank you for your hospitality but we must leave now. Thank you again." He turned to Ann and asked, "Are you ready, Ann?"

Ann replied, "No, I will stay here with Harold. He has asked me to be his wife."

They all smiled. Joi said to the others, "I told you."

"You know your father," Peter replied to Joi. "We wish

you the best, Ann."

"We still have to write our contract before we get married. If you'll promise to stop back by here on your way home, we will wait for you to get back to get married. If that's okay with you, Harold."

"Whatever you want, Precious," Harold said.

Peter smiled and said, "That makes us so very happy to know you think that much of us to wait for us to get back to get married."

Ann replied, "Yes, I do care that much about the three of you. I would have never met Harold if not for you. I thank you for letting me travel with you."

Peter smiled once again and said, "You are welcome, Ann, and we will miss you."

"I'll miss your cooking most of all," Paul said and they all smiled. Then Paul said, "It's time to go. Brother Harold, thank you for everything.

"Yes, thank you, Harold" Peter and Thomas said.

"And take care of our sister," said Thomas.

"I will protect her with my life from this day forth," Harold replied.

"Peace be upon you," they said to Harold and his family.

Then Harold said, "May the God of Abraham go with you."

# Chapter 7

They had only traveled about two or three miles when Peter said, "God is blessing us already. Look what He did for Ann. Harold seems like a very nice man."

"Yes, he does," Paul agreed. "And he is blessed to have Ann for a wife."

"Can you imagine them waiting for us to get back to get married? That makes me feel very special," Thomas said.

Then Peter said, "Do you know what would make me feel special?"

"No, I don't," Thomas said. "Tell me."

Peter replied, "If I had a relationship with God like Jesus does. Can you imagine that?"

"No, I can't. Jesus is a very special man in God's eyesight. God has blessed him like no other man before him," Thomas answered.

Then Paul said, "I want to do what's right, but no matter how hard I try, I keep doing bad things to myself and my loved ones. I would like a relationship with God. I truly want to be a servant of God."

Peter then replied, "It's very hard to serve God with the things of the world pulling on you. But, if you read the Word of God and obey it, serving God becomes much easier."

"You are right, Peter," Paul said. "Starting today I will obey my God. And maybe God will take me back as His servant."

"Do you know the way to get closer to God?" Peter asked.

"How?"

"The way to get closer to God is through prayer and fasting."

"You are right again, Peter," Thomas said. "I remember Jesus fasted for 40 days and he is always praying. My grandfather said to me one day, 'God has worked more miracles through Jesus than any of His other prophets.'"

"If what we have been told about Jesus is true, Jesus has worked more miracles than all of the other prophets combined. It's nothing that Jesus has done or can't do with God's help," Paul said.

"From what I have been told, and read about God and His prophets, I started thinking, then studying the Word of God," Peter said. "I was amazed when I realized it was one power that God has never allowed any of His prophets to use. So that everyone will know that there is only One God, and there is none that has the right to be worshipped except Him and Him alone."

Thomas interrupted Peter, "What power does God keep for Himself alone?"

"The power to be able to say, 'Let there be' and it is. No one but God can make something out of nothing like God did in His creation. Man with his limited understanding is always trying to make God like His creation or make God's creation like Him.

"Once again you are right, Peter. My grandfather would always say, 'God is one and there is nothing like Him. Most men don't even know God's name," Thomas said.

"I know one thing," Paul replied, "whenever I ask God for something He always gives it to me. God has been so good to me, even when I don't deserve it."

Then Thomas said, "You know every time we start talking about something, we always end up talking about God."

"I can't talk about anything without bringing God into it because everything in this world revolves around Him. I know if I take Him out of anything, no matter how bad it seems to be in my mind, when I look at it with my spiritual eyes it becomes okay. I know that God is in control of everything in existence. When I think about anything with that in mind, it becomes okay, no matter how bad it seems," Peter replied.

Paul smiled and said, "You always have a good way of looking at things."

"I wonder what your Uncle Steve will say when he finds out about Ann getting married to Harold," Thomas said.

"Ann told me that she and my uncle were just friends," Peter said.

"Okay," Thomas replied.

The men continued on their Journey to Tyre. "I wonder if the people in Tyre will be as nice as the people in Sidon?" Paul asked.

Peter replied, "If we can find the believers when we get there, we will be alright."

"When are we going to stop to make ourselves something to eat?" Thomas asked.

Peter and Paul laughed and teased Thomas.

"All you ever want to do is eat," Paul said.

An hour later they stopped and made camp. After they gave thanks to God, they ate. Once they finished eating, they rested under a big oak tree.

"You know trees remind me of life," Paul said.

"Trees have never reminded me of life," Thomas said.

Peter smiled.

Paul started to explain, "You must know what I mean."

"No, I don't. I just told you that," Thomas said before Paul could get another word out.

Peter began to laugh and said, "Let Paul finish, Thomas. Maybe then you will know."

"I doubt it," Thomas replied.

"Go on, Paul, finish what you were saying," Peter said.

"Thank you, Peter. Thomas is always cutting me off. As I was saying, when I look at a tree, it reminds me of life because I see the trunk of the tree as starting on the straight path to God, and the branches of the tree remind me of the choices we make in life. The trunk of the tree grows straight towards heaven, But the tree has many branches going in many different directions. Some of the branches of the tree are strong but most are weak. The strong branches represent the right choice that we make in our lives."

"I still don't fully understand," Thomas said.

"Well," said Paul, "Imagine the trunk of the tree as the Word of God. Imagine all the branches as the choices you make in life. Do you understand now, Thomas?"

"I think so," said Thomas.

"I want you to fully understand."

"Well, explain more about the branches, if you can," Thomas replied.

Paul answered, "Okay, most of the time when we are faced with a choice in our lives we know what's right, whether we do the right thing or not, we know. But sometimes we don't know what is right or wrong."

"Let me be sure I understand what you are saying," Thomas said. "If I make the wrong choice, not knowing, will I still be out on the weak branch? If the weak branch can't hold me, I will fall."

"You almost have it," Paul replied. "Ignorance of the law is an excuse with God. So, in a way you're right, Thomas. But I believe if you make a mistake and forget, God will not punish you. If you go out onto the weak branch because you forgot or made a mistake God will not let you fall. He will allow us to get back to the trunk of the tree safely. For the one who knows and willingly goes out onto the weak branch will fall. If they are a true believer and fall, they will get back up, brush themselves off, and start back up the tree."

Then Peter said, "I understand what you're saying Paul, but I believe when you don't know what's right or wrong, the best thing to do is pray to God for help to make the right choice. Then step out onto the branch on blind faith. Because we know that God can strengthen the weakest branch to hold you. God can do anything that He wants. God is great, even a blind man can see that. I see what you're talking about, Paul. I also can see the tree now in my mind. Thank you for helping me to see the tree."

Paul replied, "Don't thank me, thank God. It's time to go now."

They left and continued to talk as they traveled. By the time they approached Tyre, it was just getting dark. As they entered Tyre, Peter said, "It's very quiet around here."

"Yes, it is, and where are all the people?" remarked Thomas.

Peter said, "If you stop talking, maybe I can hear something."

"Hear what?" Thomas asked.

"I think I hear people to my right," Peter said.

"All of the houses to your right are dark inside," Paul said.

"I hear people praying to my right," Peter said.

Paul replied, "Let's go to the end of the road and look around." When they reached the end of the road, they looked to the right and left. Thomas and Paul said, "It's nothing here, Peter."

Peter replied, "Now I hear them praying behind us."

"What's going on, Peter?" Thomas asked. "One minute they're on our right, and the next minute they're behind us. We don't see anyone. This is getting spooky."

"Look around good," Peter said.

"Okay, we are looking," Paul said. "Over here."

When Thomas reached the place where Paul was standing, he said, "You're right again, Peter. There is a synagogue behind the houses."

"Should we go in, Peter?" Paul asked.

"Yes," Peter answered. "There's no better place to meet people than in the house of God. And we should bow down with those who bow down."

"I wish you could see this, Peter," Paul said. "This synagogue is longer than nine houses. I don't know what kind of stones they used, but the whole synagogue is glistening from the moonlight shining on it. It's so beautiful."

Thomas opened the door to the synagogue. "The synagogue is full," he said to Paul and Peter. They went inside, and after the religious service was over, people came over and welcomed them. One of the men welcomed them to Tyre and asked what brought them to town. Peter explained they were on their way to find Jesus.

The man said, "I have heard of him. Are you trying to

find him to get your sight?"

"Yes," Peter answered.

We have heard many stories about Jesus," the man said. "They say that Jesus has worked many miracles and he can force out demons from people."

"We have heard the same stories," Peter replied.

Just then some Sadducees overheard them talking. One of the Sadducees said, "This man called Jesus can force demons out of people only with the help of Beelzebub, the ruler of demons."

When Peter heard that, he became furious. "I was told a story about Jesus and I didn't know why Jesus said what he said. Now I do. Jesus said to some Pharisees, 'Any kingdom divided against itself will not last.' If Satan forces Satan out, he is divided against himself, so how can his kingdom last. And you say I force demons out of people with the help of Beelzebub, then who helps your followers force demons out? That's why they will be your judges. But if I force demons out with the help of God's Spirit, then the kingdom of God has come to you!"

Then the Sadducee said, "These strangers don't know anything about the man called Jesus. They only know what people have told them."

"Yes, that is true," Peter replied. "All we know about Jesus is what we have been told. But, we do know from what we have been told that he is always trying to bring the people back to the Word of God. I have never heard of Jesus saying or doing anything bad."

Another Sadducee replied, "Who are you to say what is bad or not bad? Do you know who we are? How dare you try to tell us what is good or bad. Get out of here right now."

"Let's go," Paul said and they left out of the synagogue.

Once they were outside, Thomas said with sarcasm, "Good going, Peter. You just got us thrown out of the synagogue. And what did you say, Peter? The best place to meet people is where? Also, didn't you say if we found the believers we would be okay? So, tell me what's really going on."

Peter answered, "So are you saying that we should have said nothing? Should I have just stood there and let them tell lies on Jesus. Jesus was not there to defend himself, so I did."

"I was just kidding," Thomas said. "You did the right thing."

A man approached them and said, "Peace be upon you, brothers."

"And peace be upon you," they replied.

"You are one of the men that we were talking to in the synagogue," Paul said.

"Yes, my name is Samuel, son of Minerver, but my friends call me Sam. You brothers will stay at my house tonight. Come, let's go."

"Thank you, Samuel," Peter and the others said.

When they reached Samuel's house, he said, "One minute, brothers. I must go in and make sure my daughters are decent."

"I wonder how many daughters he has," Thomas said to Peter and Paul.

Samuel returned and said, "Come in, brothers. My daughters are not at home." So they went in and Samuel offered them to sit and make themselves at home.

They thanked him and complimented his home.

"God has been good to me," Samuel said. "My daughters

should be home soon. When they get here they will make you something to eat. You must not judge all of us by what the Sadducees said. Most of us believe that Jesus is a prophet sent to us from the One God, like John the Baptist. The Sadducees and Pharisees don't like John either."

"Why?" Paul asked.

Samuel answered, "Because John and Jesus always tell the truth. That is one thing they do not like. And another thing is most of the Sadducees and Pharisees love having power over the people. They know if the people listened to John and Jesus, they would lose the power over the people. You see, here in Tyre the Pharisees and Sadducees are the ones who exercise power and have authority over the people to maintain what is just and right. But Jesus is telling the people the Sadducees and Pharisees are not giving them justice. That will take away their power and authority."

Just then the door opened and Samuel's daughters entered. They greeted the guest and their father.

"These are my daughters, Natalie, Hope, and Minerva, Minerva is named after her mother." He turned to the guest and said, "These are my guests, Peter, Thomas, and Paul. Would you prepare something to eat for them?"

"Yes, Father, we will go right now," said Hope.

"Thank you," Samuel said.

There was a knock on the door.

"I wonder who that could be this time of night. Excuse me, brothers."

Samuel got up and went to the door. When he opened the door and recognized the visitors, he invited them inside. "I believe you have met my guests."

"Yes, we have. That is why we have come."

"What do you mean?" Samuel asked.

Then one of the Sadducees said, "These strangers will cause trouble here. They must go. Now! They are not welcome in Tyre."

"These men are my guests," Samuel replied.

Then another Sadducee said, "Do you dare question our authority?"

Samuel answered, "This is my house. You or no one else on earth has authority in my house!"

The head of the Sadducees said, "See, this is what we are talking about. We knew that these strangers would cause trouble."

Then Samuel said, "It's not the strangers who came into my house and tried to take over."

The Sadducees became angry and said, "We will ask you one more time, Samuel. Send the strangers away now!"

"No, I will not," Sam replied. "These brothers are my guests. If you keep disrespecting me in my house by telling me who I can have in it, I will ask you to leave."

One of the Sadducees said, "You should remember you live here. When the strangers leave, and they *will* leave, you will still be here with us."

Samuel replied, "Who do you really think you are to come into my house and threaten me? As a matter of fact, I think it would be better for me if you all left before I say something that I shouldn't say."

One of the Sadducees said, "We were only trying to tell you."

Samuel cut him off in the middle of his statement. "Please don't say any more. Just leave. I will get the door for you."

Another of the Sadducees started to say something, but

Samuel stopped him also and said, "No. Don't say anything but goodnight."

"Goodnight," they said, and Samuel closed the door.

Then Peter said, "We are sorry for any trouble we have caused."

Samuel replied, "No, you brothers have not done anything to be sorry for. The only thing you did was tell the truth about Jesus and defend his good name. Don't bother worrying about me or yourselves. God will take care of us."

"I seek refuge with the Lord of men, the King of men, the God of men. From the whispering of the evil one who whispers into the hearts of men from among men, "Peter said."

"That's what I say when evil people talk to me or when evil thoughts come into my head." Samuel said.

"That's a powerful prayer. I must remember it," Paul said.

"Father, the food is ready," said Hope.

Samuel thanked his daughter and invited the men to come and eat. After their meal, the men thanked them.

"You all are welcome," Samuel said. "Hope is the youngest but an excellent cook. She takes after her mother in that way."

"She will make a good wife to someone someday," Thomas said.

"Yes, she will," Samuel replied. "All of my daughters are blessed with one or more good qualities of their mother. My daughter, Natalie, has her mother's beauty on the inside and outside. My oldest daughter, Minerva, is very smart in many ways just like her mother was. But they are my daughters. Someone else may disagree with me about who is the best cook, and who is the prettiest, or the smartest. But I believe whichever of my daughters a man takes for a wife she will do the best she can to make and keep him happy.

Then Thomas said, "From the little I have seen of your daughters I also believe that any man would be blessed with either one of them."

"Thank you very much," Samuel said. "That was a nice thing to say. You brothers must be tired. I will take you to your room."

"Thank you, we are tired," Peter said.

Samuel took them to their room and said goodnight. Once they were settled in the room, Peter said to Thomas and Paul, "See, we did find a friend in the house of God. God has always sent someone to help in my time of need."

"You're right," Paul said. "If I ever needed anything, whether it was earthly or spiritual, God always sent help to me."

"Hope is a very beautiful young woman and she can cook well too," Thomas said.

"It sounds like you have eyes for Hope," Paul said and Peter agreed.

Thomas replied, "I don't know what you're talking about. I was just trying to say that Hope is a nice young woman and she cooks good. That's all I meant. I hope Samuel will be okay when we leave."

"Samuel is a servant of God. God will protect him," Peter replied.

"I know God will take care of Samuel, but he will be here all alone," Thomas said. "Maybe one of us should stay here with him for a little while."

Peter and Paul looked at each other and smiled. Peter said, "I guess if someone has to stay with Samuel it should be you, right?"

"I will if Paul doesn't want to," Thomas replied. "You know it's the right thing to do since we are responsible for the Sadducees being angry with him."

"You're right. We are responsible for them being angry with Samuel, and Hope has nothing to do with someone staying here," Peter answered.

Paul answered, "Oh no, Hope has nothing to do with anyone staying." Peter and Paul began to laugh.

"Go on and laugh," Thomas said. "But I will say it again, Hope has nothing to do with it."

"Let's go to sleep," Peter said.

"Yes, let's go to sleep," Thomas replied.

# Chapter 8

A little before daybreak Peter heard Samuel calling them to come for prayer. They went downstairs and joined Samuel and his family. Following the prayer, the aroma of food cooking spread throughout the house.

"That food sure smells good," Paul said.

"Yes, it does smell good," Thomas replied. "Maybe Hope is cooking."

Once the food was prepared, they went in to eat. During the meal Thomas complimented Hope on how very good the food was. Hope smiled and thanked him. He then introduced himself by name to Hope. Everyone looked at Thomas and smiled, including Samuel. Just then there was a knock at the door.

"I wonder who that could be this early in the morning?" Samuel said. "Excuse me, brothers." Sam got up from the table and went to answer the door.

When Sam opened the door, there stood what appeared to be about thirty men outside. He greeted them and asked what he could do for them. One of the men quickly spoke up.

"We came to let you know that you are not alone."

"Thank you, brothers," said Samuel.

Another one of the men said, "We know some of the Sadducees came to your house last night. We didn't know what happened, so we came as soon as we could to make sure you were alright."

Samuel replied, "I thank God for you all. Please come in."

"We thank God for you also, and thank you for inviting us in, but we have to go to work now. We will be back to check on you after work."

"Okay," said Samuel. "Peace be upon you, my brothers."

"And peace and blessings be upon you, my brother," they said.

Samuel closed the door and went back into the house and rejoined his family and guests. "See, I told you, brothers, many of us in Tyre believe that Jesus is a man sent to us from God, and that was not all of us who believe that Jesus is a prophet. There are many more. If you brothers stay a little longer, God willing, you will meet them all."

"We were talking last night about one of us staying here with you," Peter said. "But now we know it's not necessary, so we will all leave as soon as we finish talking. On our way back home, we will stop back here and meet all of the believers, if it be God's will."

"Now that we know you're not going to be alone, we can leave and not worry about you. We are happy that you have so many brothers to fellowship with," Paul said.

"This has nothing to do with what we are talking about," Thomas said. "But I must say this now. Brother Samuel, I have feelings for Hope. I want to take Hope for my wife, with your permission."

"Go on, brother," Samuel replied, encouraging Thomas to continue talking.

"I really don't know what else to say," Thomas admitted.

"Say what's on your heart," Samuel said.

"As I said before, I believe that Hope would make any man

a good wife. I don't have much, but I will share everything I have with her. That is my word to you. I will treat her like a gift from God always. That is my word to God also."

Samuel replied, "I would be honored to have you for a son, but I don't know how Hope feels. I will ask her if she feels the same way about you. You must excuse me, I have to go talk to Hope now. I will be back shortly."

After Samuel left the room, Peter said, "Thomas, do you know what you're doing? You just met her and you don't know anything about her."

"I know exactly what I want," Thomas said. "I want Hope for my wife. I pray to God that she wants me too."

"Peter is right, Thomas. You don't know anything about her."

"I know that Hope believes in the One God like I do. I know that she respects and obeys her father. A woman who respects and obeys her father will respect and obey her husband. That's what I know about Hope and that's enough for me, so don't say anything else about me asking for her hand in marriage."

Samuel went to Hope's bedroom to speak with her. After knocking on the door, she invited him in. "I need to talk to you about something important," he said.

"What is it Father?" Hope asked.

"Well, baby, Thomas has asked me for your hand in marriage."

Her eyes lit up. "God is good. But Father, what should I do?"

I can't make that decision for you. You are a woman now. Yes, I know many things about life and marriage, but I don't know what's in a person's heart. Only God knows that and that's what's most important. What's in his heart?

I do know that Thomas believes in the One God like we do, and I believe he will do his best to protect you from all of the evils of this world."

"Father, I like Thomas, but I do not love him," Hope said.

"Do you love God?" asked Samuel.

"Yes, Father."

"I did not love your mother when we got married, and we had a good happy home because the both of us loved God." Samuel continued to tell Hope about marriage. "Do you think Eve loved Adam when God first gave her to him?" he asked. "You have known Thomas longer than Eve knew Adam."

"I love you, Father. I thank God for you. You can tell Thomas I will be honored to be his wife." Hope kissed her father.

Samuel smiled and said, "I will tell Thomas the good news. This is a happy day for me also."

Samuel returned to Peter, Paul, and Thomas. Thomas was eager to hear Hope's answer.

Samuel returned. "My son, I told Hope what you asked me but I have bad news."

Thomas dropped his head and was filled with sadness.

"My daughter is leaving my house," Samuel said.

Thomas got up from the table and threw his arms around Samuel and said, "You are going to be my father-in-law."

"May God bless you and Hope," Peter said. "And keep the both of you on the straight path."

"Thank you Peter," said Thomas.

"When are you and Hope getting married?" Paul asked.

"I don't know," Thomas said. "I must ask Hope."

The others chuckled and said, "We know who will be running your house."

71

Thomas replied, "Yes, Hope will run our home and everything else that she has the right to run. I will give my wife all the rights that God says that a wife should have and more. I will give her some of my part too, if it keeps peace."

Samuel smiled and said, "My son's marriage will last. Thomas, you are a wise man for your age. I say that because a wise man's main focus is to maintain peace in his home, because he knows if he can't even keep peace in his house then how can he keep peace any place else. The more I learn about you, Thomas, the more I thank God for you honoring my household by marrying my daughter."

"The honor is all mine and I also thank God for blessing me to be a part of your household. Brother Samuel, may I talk to Hope now?"

Samuel gave him permission to talk to Hope, and told him where her bedroom was located.

Thomas went to Hope's room and knocked on the door. She instructed him to come in. When he went into her room he found her standing by the window with the biggest smile on her face. They greeted one another and Thomas stepped further into the room.

"My father told me what you asked him," Hope said.

"You look so beautiful standing there with the sun shining on your face," Thomas said, smiling.

"Thank you. No one but my father has ever called me beautiful."

"I will be the best husband that I can be to you, Hope."

"I believe you will," said Hope.

"I came to ask you two things," Thomas said.

"What is it, Thomas?"

"When would you like to get married?"

"Whenever you want will be okay with me," Hope replied.

Thomas was so relieved when Hope said that. "Your answer to the first question makes the second question so much easier for me. You know we were on our way to find Jesus, so I would like to wait until we get back from finding Jesus to get married, if that's okay with you."

"That's fine with me," Hope said. "I will be here waiting on the day when you get back to me. I want you to do what God has put on your heart to do. My first job as a wife is to help you do what God tells you to do."

"You make me and God proud," Thomas said.

"Thank you for saying that," Hope replied. "I hope I will always please God and you for the rest of my life."

"You're a good woman, Hope, and I know we will be happy together."

"Yes, we will," said Hope.

"We are getting ready to leave now. I will miss you every minute that we are gone."

"I will wait for you, Thomas," Hope said. They hugged and Thomas took her hand and kissed it and left her room.

"Thomas tries his best to please doesn't he?" Samuel said to Peter.

"Yes, he does," said Peter. "Thomas has grown a lot in the last few weeks."

"I will miss Thomas traveling with us," Paul said.

"I will miss him also," said Peter. "First, we lost Ann, and now we are losing Thomas."

"You still have me. I will never leave you," Paul said. "We will find Jesus together, with God's help."

"Neither will I leave you, until we find Jesus," said

Thomas. "Are you brothers ready to go?"

Peter replied, "Yes, we are ready. Thank you, Samuel, for everything."

"Father, I will be back," Thomas said to Samuel. "I have talked to Hope. We have decided to wait until I get back to get married."

"Good," Samuel said. "May the God of Abraham guide your footsteps back to us."

Thomas replied, "Thank you, and may God keep you and your family safe until I return."

"Peace and blessings be upon you, brothers," Samuel said.

# Chapter 9

"Where are we headed, Paul?" Thomas asked.

"We are going to Galilee. It's about fifty miles away," Paul replied.

"It looks like it's going to rain," Thomas said.

"We could go to Ptolemais, it's only about 10 miles away," Paul suggested.

"That sounds like a good idea," Peter and Thomas said.

"Okay, Ptolemais it is." Paul said.

"You know you surprised me, Thomas. I thought you were going to stay there with Hope," said Peter.

Thomas replied, "We started this journey together and we will finish it together."

"I already have a wife, so there is nothing to make me leave you, Peter," Paul said.

"I really miss, Ann," Peter said. The others agreed. While they were walking, the rain started to fall. By the time they reached Ptolemais they were soaking wet. Paul pointed out an Inn ahead of them. They went into the Inn.

The innkeeper welcomed them. "You must be Peter, and one of you brothers must be Thomas, and the other is Paul? Am I right?" said the innkeeper.

The three of them were surprised that the innkeeper knew their names.

Peter asked the innkeeper, "How do you know our names?"

"Oh, forgive me. My name is Scotty and this is my Inn. I have your room ready."

Paul said, "You didn't answer the question. How do you know our names and why do you have a room for us?"

Scotty then said, "A young woman came in a few hours ago. She told me that three men would be coming and for me to hold a room for you. She also told me one of the men could not see. She paid for your room and food."

Thomas looked at Paul and said, "It must be Hope. She must have known a short cut to the Inn."

"Yes, it must be Hope," said Paul.

The innkeeper then said, "She didn't tell me her name and I forgot to ask."

Suddenly an upstairs door opened and there she stood with the biggest smile on her face. "Peace be upon you, brothers."

"But how did you know we would be here?" Thomas asked.

"God put it on my heart where to find you," she said.

"We thought we would not see you again for at least a few months," Paul said.

"I could not sleep at night for thinking about you. So, here I stand. God is great," she said.

"Yes, He is, Ann," Peter said. "We were just talking about you today. We were saying how much we missed you."

Ann smiled and said, "I know Thomas has missed my cooking."

"Wait until we tell you about Thomas," Paul said, smiling.

"What about Thomas? Tell me," Ann said.

"Come, let's go sit down and talk," Peter said. "First, how are you, Ann, and how is Harold?"

"The both of us are okay, thank God. How are you

brothers?"

"We are fine," Peter replied. It's so good to hear your voice again."

"I have missed you also, Peter," said Ann. "Now tell me about Thomas. What is going on?"

"I want to be the one to give you the good news," Paul said. "You're not the only one getting married."

"Congratulations, Peter," Ann said.

"No, it's not me who is getting married," Peter said. "It's Thomas."

"Oh, congratulations, Thomas. She must be a very good cook."

They all laughed and Thomas said, "Yes, Hope is a very good cook."

"How and where did you meet her?" Ann asked.

"I met her in Tyre. We stayed at her father's house. You will like her. She's a good woman like you," Thomas said.

"You're so sweet, Thomas," Ann said, and then turned to Peter. "So, Peter, how have you been doing?"

Thomas quickly said, "Oh, Peter has been doing just fine. But did you know that Peter caused us to be thrown out of a synagogue?"

"What?" Ann said.

"Don't start that again, Thomas," Paul said.

Thomas smiled and said, "Well, he did. And what do you mean by don't start again?"

"What is Thomas talking about?" Ann asked.

"This is what happened," Paul said. "When we were in Tyre there were some Sadducees in the synagogue. They were saying bad things about Jesus and Peter spoke up in Jesus' defense. The Sadducees became very angry and told all of us to get out of the synagogue."

"Good for you, Peter," said Ann. "We should never let anyone say anything bad about God or His prophets in our presence without defending them. Harold says we should defend God and His prophets with our hands if we can, but if we can't then we should defend them with our tongues. If we can't do it with our tongues or hands, then we should defend him in our heart. This is the least we should do, so for you to defend one of God's prophets with your tongue, God and I are proud of you, Peter."

Peter then said, "I hope so. I need God's blessing."

"I believe I can speak for all of us when I say you are a righteous man, Peter," Ann said. "And I also believe that God will help you, through Jesus."

"Yes, I believe that God will help me through Jesus also. Ann, it is so good to have you back and not just for your cooking."

"I feel good about being back with you brothers too."

"Is it time to eat now?" Thomas asked.

"Yes, we can eat now, Thomas," Ann replied. While they were eating, Ann asked Thomas to tell her about Hope.

"I don't know where to start," Thomas said. "Hope believes in the One God like we do. And she is very supportive of me doing what God wants me to do. She will be a good wife to me in every way. I don't know a lot about her, but what I do know about her I love!"

"She sounds like a good woman," Ann said.

"She is," Thomas replied. "Hope is like you in a lot of ways."

"Look out here," Paul said. "Who are all of those people coming?"

Ann said, "Look out of this window. You can see them all. It's so many of them and they are coming this way."

Everyone in the inn ran to the door and looked out. "We are being attacked."

The Innkeeper sounded the alarm. When the men of the town heard the battle alarm they came running and formed a battle line to fight the invaders. As the people came closer to the town, one of the men said, "That's not an army. They have children with them."

"You're right," said the leader of the town. Put your weapons away." When the people reached the town, the leader of the town said, "Peace be upon you."

The leader of the people said, "Peace be upon you all and may God bless you."

The town's leader asked, "Where are you coming from, and where are you going?"

"We are from Beirut. We are going to Galilee."

"For what?" the Innkeeper asked.

"Did you know that King Herod has put John the Baptist in prison?"

"No, I didn't."

"King Herod's birthday is three weeks from now. He is having a big celebration for his birthday. We plan to cry out for John's freedom during the celebration. Maybe King Herod will be in a good spirit and free him."

Then Peter said to Ann and the others, "Maybe we should go with them to Galilee and try to free John also. They all agreed.

"My grandfather told me that Jesus and John the Baptist are cousins," Thomas said. "Maybe Jesus will be there."

"Maybe so," Paul said. "But, it's more important that we get John out of prison."

The leader of the town said to the leaders of the travelers, "Your people must be tired and hungry. They can rest here, and we will bring you some food."

"Thank you, and may the One God bless you all for your kindness." He then turned to his people and said, "We will rest here tonight."

The elder leader of the travelers said to the leader of the town, "I thank God first for everything in life, the good and the bad. Nothing in life happens without God's permission, this I believe. I do ask God to bless you all."

The town's leader replied, "You are right. Thanks, and all praise is due to God, the Lord of the worlds. We must be careful not to give man or anything God's praise or his thanks. We must protect ourselves from men trying to give us what belongs to God. Like when men call you good or thank you for something. We should say don't thank me, but thank God for blessing me so that I could help you. When they call you good, you should say, there is only One that is good and that is God!"

"You are blessed beyond your years," the old man said.

"I know a little about God's word, but more than most. God has blessed me to see things that most people can't see," he replied.

The women brought food to the travelers. When Thomas saw it, he asked if they could go back inside to eat. They all agreed to go inside. Once they finished eating, Peter said, "So many things are happening on this trip."

"You are right," Thomas said. "Now we are on our way to Galilee, not to find Jesus, but to help free John the Baptist."

"That's okay," said Ann. "That's how life is. You start out on a journey to do one thing and life has you doing so many other things before you do what you set out to do. Sometimes you don't get to do what you started out to do. But remember God is in control of everything. Everything will work out for the glory of God. So, just thank God for allowing us to be a part of His masterplan."

"That's what I love about you, Ann," Thomas said. "You always have the words to help us look at things in the right way. I thank God for sending you back to us."

"You are so sweet, Thomas. Hope will be blessed to have you for a husband. How was the food?"

"Well, it was not as good as Hope's. Oh... or yours, Ann."

"You got out of that, Thomas," Paul said, smiling.

Peter suggested they go lay down and rest. The men agreed. Ann decided to stay behind. While she was sitting outside the inn, a little girl came to her and introduced herself as Pearl. Ann introduced herself to the little girl and they began talking.

"My mother is taking me to Galilee," Pearl said. "I've never been to Galilee before. Have you?"

"Yes, I have," Ann answered. "It's a big city, you will like it there."

"I don't think so," Pearl answered shaking her head.

"Why?"

"Because my mother said the king of Galilee is bad, and I don't like bad people. The king might hurt me and my mother. Are you afraid of the king?" Pearl asked.

"No," Ann replied. "If I was afraid, I would sing one of the songs of David."

"Who is David?" Pearl asked.

"David was Israel's second king. David loved God," Ann said.

"I love God too," Pearl said. "What song do you sing when you're afraid?"

"I will teach you the song. I will say the words and I want you to sing them." Ann started saying the words to the 23rd

Psalm. After a few verses, Pearl began to sing. Once Pearl finished the song, Ann asked her if she was still afraid to go to Galilee.

"No," Pearl replied. "That song is so beautiful. Could we sing some more?"

"Don't you think your mother might be looking for you?"

"Maybe," Pearl answered. "Let's sing some more of the song, please."

Ann said, "I'll tell you what, I have a friend named Peter and he has one of the most beautiful voice you have ever heard. I will get him to sing for you later. But, you must go to your mother now."

"Okay, I'll see you later."

"You have a beautiful voice," the innkeeper said to Ann as he stood in the doorway.

"I love singing to God, whether it's to thank Him or to ask him for help. God blessed me with this voice. I want to always praise him with my voice."

"Are you and your friends really going to Galilee to ask the king to free John the Baptist?"

"Yes, we are."

"Why?" The innkeeper asked.

"Because, I believe that John is a prophet of God. If we can help him, God will be pleased with us. If we go and cannot help him, God will still be pleased with us for trying. Any way you look at it, if we go to Galilee, God will be pleased with us."

"You make me want to close up my inn and go too," the innkeeper said.

"You should. We need everyone that believes that John the Baptist is a prophet of God to be there."

"I can't close the inn. I will lose a lot of money."

"Money is not everything," Ann said.

"Money isn't everything, but I need it to live."

"That's what Satan wants us to believe. Before there was any money, we survived. Don't forget who takes care of you."

"You are right," the innkeeper said. "There was a time when I didn't have any money for seven months and God didn't let the owner of my home throw me out. I also had food every day. We don't need money, all we need is belief in God. Thank you, I will go with you to Galilee."

# Chapter 10

"**A**nn, where are you?" Peter called out.

"Right over here, Peter," Ann replied.

"I can't sleep. I have been thinking about us going to Galilee."

"I hope King Herod will free John," Ann said.

"I hope so too, but we must remember the story about King Herod's father."

"What story?" Ann asked.

"I thought everyone who believed that Jesus was sent to us from God knew that story. The story goes, an angel of the Lord appeared to Joseph, the husband of Mary, the mother of Jesus in a dream and said, 'Get up and take the child and his mother and flee to Egypt. Stay there until God tells you, because Herod intends to find the child and kill him.' So Joseph got up and woke Mary and said we are leaving. They left for Egypt. They stayed in Egypt until they heard that Herod had died. God had saved Jesus from Herod. Maybe God will save John from King Herod, too."

"God will do what's right for John, just as He will do what's right for all of us," Ann said. "This I believe with all of my heart and soul."

"I thank God for righteous women, and you are a righteous woman Ann," Peter said.

"I thank God for blessing me with the will to obey His word, Peter. Oh, I met a little girl named Pearl. She is so sweet and smart. I promised her something that I maybe shouldn't have promised her. I promised her that you would sing a song for her."

"Why did you do that?" Peter asked.

"I sang a few verses to her, and then I told her about you and your angelic voice."

Peter smiled. "I will do it for you."

Ann thanked him. She then told him she had encouraged the innkeeper to go with them to Galilee. Peter wanted to know what would happen to the inn if the innkeeper traveled with them. She explained to him that he would close down the inn until he came back from Galilee.

Moments later, Ann heard a child's voice call her name. she turned and found Pearl approaching.

"Miss Ann," the little girl called out. "My mother wants to meet you. I told her about you and she told me to ask you if you would come to meet her."

"I would love to meet your mother," Ann replied.

When Pearl heard her answer, her smile grew bigger. She took Ann by the hand and said, "Come on, let's go," pulling her. They walked through the camp and when they reached Pearl's mother she was cooking.

"Peace be upon you, sister," Pearl's mother said.

"And peace and blessings be upon you, my sister. May the God of Abraham have mercy on you," Ann replied.

"Come sit down and break bread with us."

"Thank you. I will be happy to."

"Thank you for being kind to my daughter."

"You're welcome, but it was Pearl that was nice to me. You're doing a good job raising her."

Pearl's mother smiled and thanked Ann. "I try very hard to teach her right from wrong and to have respect for everyone."

"Is your husband traveling with you?" Ann asked.

With sadness, Pearl's mother replied, "My husband died five years ago."

"It's always sad when we lose a loved one, but remember God brings people into our life and He takes them out. We have no say over who comes into our life or goes out. We just have to thank God for the time we had with them. A minute of happiness is better than no happiness at all. So I always thank God for everyone that He brings into my life, and when He takes them out. I know it must be hard raising a little girl alone."

"No, it's not hard because God has blessed me to live in a small village. All of the people in the village are helping me raise Pearl to be a true believer in God, and I thank God everyday for that."

"Yes, God is so good to us, because we believe and praise Him and Him alone," Ann replied.

"Pearl told me that you are going to Galilee with us."

"Yes," Ann replied. "Me and my friends are going."

"Which of the three men is your husband, Ann?"

"Neither of them. They are my friends. A true friend is a blessing from God. After we find Jesus I will return to Sidon to be married to one of the kindest men that I have ever met in my life."

"That is good. Tell me, Ann, why are you and your friends looking for Jesus?"

"It is said there were two blind men following Jesus, shouting, 'Have mercy on us, Son of David.' Jesus went into a house, and the blind men followed him. Jesus said to them, 'Do you believe that I can do this?' They answered, 'Yes.' So Jesus touched their eyes and said what you have believed will be done for you. After that they could see. Jesus warned them, 'Don't let anybody know about this,' but they went out and spread the news about Jesus throughout the region. So my friend, Peter, who is blind, believes that with God Jesus can give him sight too."

Pearl's mother said, "I hope your friend will be given the desire of his heart, and be able to see."

"I think it's time for me to go back to the inn now. Thank you for the food. I don't know your name."

"My name is Pye."

Well, Pye, I hope to see you later."

The women said goodbye to each other and Ann departed. When she reached the inn, Paul, Thomas, and Peter were sitting down talking. She greeted them and sat down with them.

"We just heard that Jesus is in Jericho," Paul said. "So, we have decided not to go to Galilee, but to go to Jericho instead."

"What do you mean, we have decided? I haven't decided anything," Ann said.

"We *are* looking for Jesus, right?" Thomas said.

"Yes, but one of God's prophets is in prison. Maybe we can help him. What do you have to say about it, Peter?" asked Ann.

"First, please forgive us, Ann," Peter said. "We shouldn't have made any decision without you. You're right, it's more important that we go to Galilee and try to free John."

"Peter, I know how much finding Jesus means to you. God will bless you for going to Galilee," Ann said.

"Ann, life has many tests," said Peter. "I would have failed this one if you were not here with us."

"Ann, what do you know about John the Baptist?" Thomas asked.

"Not much," she admitted. "But I can share with you what I've been told. He was preaching and baptizing in the wilderness of Judea for the people to turn back to God and repent for the kingdom of heaven is near. They say he wears clothes made from camel's hair with a leather belt around his waist. He only eats locusts and wild honey. All of Judea and the whole Jordan Valley go to him. One day when the people were confessing their sins, John the Baptist saw many of the Pharisees and Sadducees coming to be baptized. John said to them, 'You deadly snakes, who showed you how to flee from God's coming anger? Do those things that prove you have turned to God and have changes in the way you think and act. Don't think you can say Abraham is our ancestor. I can guarantee that God can raise up descendants for Abraham from these stones. The ax is now to cut the roots of the trees. Any tree that doesn't produce good fruit will be cut down and thrown into a fire. I baptize you with water so that you will change the way you think and act, but the one who comes after me is more powerful than I. He will baptize you with the Holy Spirit and fire. He will clean up his threshing floor. He will gather his wheat into barns, but the husks in a fire, that can never be put out.' That's all I know about John the Baptist."

A man was standing behind them. He interrupted them and said, "Excuse me. I overheard you talking about John the Baptist. "I was baptized by John the Baptist. I have been following him for a few years. My name is John also, and I was told that Jesus said 'There is no one who has been born from a woman that is greater than John the Baptist.'"

"You must know a lot about him," Thomas said.

"He is like no man I have ever met or heard about. He

has many followers that would give him anything he asks for, but he refuses to accept anything from anyone but God."

"Most holy men that I know are always asking for money," Thomas said.

John replied, "Out of all the holy men I know, John the Baptist is the only one that doesn't take money from the people. He could be rich. The people love him. They will do anything he tells them to do. John the Baptist is not an ordinary person; he is truly a prophet of God. All he wants out of life is to preach the Word of God to the true believers. He is not like the Sadducees and Pharisees who are taken care of very well and want for nothing. No one can say that they take care of John the Baptist, but God. And that's the way John wants it."

"Tell us why Herod put John in prison," said Paul.

"Because John spoke out against Herod taking his brother's wife."

"That's not a reason to have him arrested," Paul said.

"King Herod did it for Herodias, the wife of his brother, Phillip."

"Why would Herodias want John arrested?" Peter asked.

"Because John has been telling Herod it was not right for him to marry his brother's wife. You see, John is not afraid to tell the truth. He never lies, unlike the Sadducees and Pharisees. They sometimes bend the truth because they depend on the people to take care of them, like King Herod does."

"I see now why he doesn't take anything from anyone but God," Ann said. "Because whoever takes care of you is your master."

"That's one way of looking at it," said John.

"John, when will you be leaving for Galilee?" Peter asked.

"Right after our dawn prayer, if God wills," John answered.

Then Thomas went to the innkeeper and asked, "Could you bring us some food?"

The innkeeper replied, "What would you like me to bring?"

Thomas answered, "Bring us a little of everything."

Ann interrupted, "Thomas, what are you doing?"

"Ordering food," Thomas answered. "We are celebrating."

"What are we celebrating?" Paul asked.

"Making the right decision," Thomas responded.

"Thomas always can find a reason to eat," Peter said.

They all laughed. Thomas smiled and said, "So, I guess none of you wants to eat?"

Paul smiled and said, "If you are paying, we are eating." They all laughed again. The innkeeper brought them the food. After they had been eating, John thanked Thomas for the food.

When they finished eating, Thomas said, "My bed is calling me."

"Mine too," said John.

"I guess we are all going to bed," said Paul.

"Not me and you, Peter. We have to go see Pearl first." The two of them left.

When they reached Pearl and her mother, the little girl started jumping up and down.

"What would you like me to sing for you, Pearl?"

"I don't know the name of the song," said Pearl, "but Miss Ann does."

In Search of Jesus the Christ

Peter turned to Ann and asked which song she was talking about.

"The song of David's deliverance," Ann said.

"Oh, that song," Peter said and began to sing. Many people in the village heard him and gathered around. Pye looked like she had been taken away to another world. The smile on her face was heavenly as she listened to Peter. Peter loved sharing his gift from God with the world. He started singing another song. Hours passed by. Ann had to stop him from singing because the time was late.

Ann asked Peter, "How long would you have song if I had not stopped you?"

"I don't know," Peter replied. "When I hear people clapping, it's like I can see them. I know you don't understand. As long as I hear people clapping and shouting, the more I will sing. I have never sung as long as I would like to for people. One day I will sing until I cannot sing anymore. I love it. God has blessed me in so many ways." A tear rolled down his face.

Ann saw the tear and said, "Yes, God has blessed you in many ways, but the most important gift God has given you is your heart. Come on, it is time to go."

Then Ann said, "Peter, what did you think about Pye?"

"Who is Pye?" Thomas asked.

"She is the little girl's mother," Peter replied.

"So Peter, what did you think about her?" Ann asked again. "She needs a husband."

Thomas and Paul looked at each other with a puzzled look.

"Well, she does have a little girl to raise," Peter said.

"Oh, that's why Peter was singing," Thomas said.

"No," Peter replied. "Ann asked me to sing for Pearl, not

91

her mother, right, Ann?"

Ann smiled and said, "Yes, I did. But you haven't answered my question. What did you think about Pye?"

Peter answered, "I didn't say more than two words to her, and she didn't say anything to me."

Thomas said. "Ann is trying to find you a wife, Peter."

"I want to find Jesus, not a wife," Peter replied.

"I was not trying to find a husband either, but I did," Ann said.

Then Thomas said, "I wasn't trying to find a wife, but I did also."

"Good for the both of you," said Peter. "All I want to do is go to Galilee and to find Jesus. That's it."

With a smile on her face, Ann said, "Well, you know Pearl and her mother are going with us to Galilee and to find Jesus also. Let's go." So they all left the inn.

# Chapter 11

They walked and walked looking for Pearl and her mother. Thomas wanted to know how much longer they were going to look for them.

"Not much longer," Ann said.

"Maybe it's not meant for us to find them," Thomas said.

"Miss Ann, Miss Ann."

"That's Pearl's voice," Ann said. "Over here."

Ann looked around and there was Pearl sitting on a camel. "Pearl," Ann cried.

They started making their way through the crowd to Pearl and her mother. When they reached Pearl and Pye, Ann greeted them. They all started walking together.

They talked about John the Baptist when Pye said to Peter, "Why are you going to see John the Baptist. He can't give you back your sight."

Peter asked, "How long have you been a widow?"

"For about five years. My husband was killed by a lion. Are you married?"

Peter smiled and said, "No. I haven't found anyone crazy enough to marry me."

"You shouldn't be so hard on yourself. God will send you a wife one day."

"Why haven't you remarried?" Peter asked.

"God hasn't sent me a husband yet, but He will. Pearl needs a father. I can be a mother to her, but I know that I could never be a father to her. It takes a man to be a father and no matter how hard a woman tries, she can never take the place of a man."

Peter then said, "You are right, Pye. It takes a woman and a man to raise a child. One day I will have a child to raise to be a servant of God."

Pye replied, "Children are a blessing. I don't know what I would have done without Pearl when God took my husband back."

"That's a good way of looking at death," Peter said.

"Yes, God took his servant back, but I thank God for the time He gave me with my husband. I miss him but God knows best. You see Peter, even in death, a true believer becomes closer to God."

"I understand, Pye, because God has brought many people into my life. Some for a long time, and some for a short time. Some have left, and some have died. Sometimes I feel sad when they are taken out of my life. But, as you said, God knows best. I believe that, too. A True believer would never question God about anything that happens in his life. A true believer knows that God has their best interest at heart at all times."

"You are right, Peter," said Pye.

Peter then said, "Let me tell you about a man named Job. He was one of the most faithful of the true believers. He lived in the east, in the city of Uz. He was an upright man and he loved God. He had seven sons and three daughters, and owned many sheep, goats, camels, oxen, donkeys, and also had many servants."

"It sounds like this Job was a very wealthy and important man," Pye said.

"Yes, you're right. He was the most important man in

the east. One day, the angels came to stand before the Lord, and Satan came with them. God said to Satan, 'What have you been doing?' Satan replied, 'I have been going all over the earth causing mischief among the believers.' God then said to Satan, 'Have you tried my true servant, Job?' Satan answered God saying, 'You have blessed Job and everything he has. But if you take away all that you have blessed him with, I will whisper into his heart and make him curse you to your face.' Then God said to Satan, 'I am God. I say to you, you evil one, I know what you know not. My servant, Job will never curse me. Let the test begin. Go whisper all you want, you disbeliever.' Satan then left the Lord's presence. You see, Pye, the Lord is the only one who knows man's heart. God knew that Job was a true believer."

"Go on with the story," Pye said.

Peter smiled and started back telling the story. "Men from Sheba attacked Job's servants and killed all of them but one. They took all of his oxen and donkeys. While the one who escaped was telling Job about what happened, someone else appeared and told him that the fire of God came from heaven and killed all of Job's sheep. While he was still speaking, another servant came in and said to Job, 'Your sons and daughters were at your oldest son's house when a storm came like I have never seen before. The storm struck the four corners of the house, causing the walls to collapse. Everyone in the house was killed.' Job said, 'Naked I came into the world, and naked I will return. The Lord has given and the Lord has taken away. May the name of the Lord be praised.' Job did not blame God."

Then, Pye said, "Job is a true believer to go through all of that and still believe in the God of Abraham."

"The story is not over. Listen to what happened next.

Again, there was a day when the angels came to present themselves to God, and Satan came among them again to present himself before the Lord. God said to Satan, 'Did I not tell you that I know what you know not?' Satan replied, 'Oh my Lord, if you take away Job's health, I know that he will curse you to your face.' The Lord said to Satan, 'Job is in your hands, but you must not kill him.' So Satan left the Lord's presence."

"Painful boils suddenly came over Job from his head to his feet. He was in so much pain. His wife said, 'Are you still holding on to your God? You should curse Him and die.' Job said to his wife, 'You're talking like a disbeliever. We accept the good things that God gives us and we thank Him for them. Even the disbelievers are thankful for the good things that happens to them. A true believer gives thanks for the bad things also, because they know that God knows best."

"Many days passed. Job was still in pain, still he never cursed God. A true believer knows that God always knows what's beyond man's understanding and Job was a true believer. Finally, the test was over."

"What happened after the test ended?" Pye asked.

"God restored Job's health and gave him twice the amount of possessions that he had. There is much more to the story. Maybe one day I will tell you the rest."

Pye smiled and said, "Thank you, and I would like to hear more of the story one day."

"It's about time to make camp, isn't it?" Peter asked.

"Yes, it is," Pye said. "How did you know?"

"It's not hard," said Peter. "I can feel the sun on my face.

A short time later, they made camp. "Are you hungry, Peter?" Pye asked.

"Yes," Peter answered.

"Did I hear you ask if we were hungry, Pye?" Thomas said.

Pye smiled and said, "I will cook for all of you. She cooked and gave Peter his food first. Then she fed Pearl, and she told the others they could get their food.

After they finished eating, Pearl asked Peter, "Will you sing me another song?"

Pye said, "Pearl, he just finished eating, honey."

Peter smiled and said, "It's okay. I will sing if Ann will sing with me."

"What are we going to sing?" Ann asked.

Peter replied, "King David wrote a song long ago. When I think of John the Baptist, I think of this song. You might know the song. It goes like this. *Come quickly to rescue me, O God! Come quickly to help me, O Lord! Let those who seek my life be confused and put to shame. Let those who want my downfall be turned back and disgraced. Let those who say Aha, Aha be turned back because of their own shame. Let all who love your salvation continually say, God is great! O God, come to me quickly. You are my help and my savior. O Lord, do not delay!*"

Ann stopped Peter and said, "Yes, I know it."

So Peter and Ann started singing. Much like before, people came and gathered around Peter and Ann to hear them sing. After the song was over, the people shouted, 'More, more.' Peter started singing Psalm nine.

"*I will give You thanks, oh Lord with all my heart. I will tell about all the miracles You have done. I will find joy and be glad about you. I will make music to praise your name, O Most High. When my enemies retreat, they will stumble and die in your presence. You have defended my just cause. You sat down on your throne as a fair judge. You condemned nations. You destroyed wicked people. You've wiped out their names forever and ever. The enemy is finished, in ruins forever. You have uprooted their cities. Even the memory of them has faded. Yes, the Lord is enthroned forever. He has set up his throne for judgment. He alone judges the world with righteousness. He judges its people faintly. The Lord is a stronghold for the oppressed, a stronghold in times of trouble. Those who know your name trust You, O Lord, because you have never deserted those who seek your help. Make music to praise the Lord who enthroned is Zion. Announce to the nations what He has done. The one who avenges murder has remembered oppressed people. He has never forgotten their cries. Have pity on me, O Lord. Look at what I suffer because of those who hate me. You take me away from the gates of death so that I may recite your praises one by one in the gates of Zion and find joy in your salvation. The nations have sunk into the pit they have made. Their feet are caught in the net they have hidden to trap others. The Lord is known by the judgment He has carried out. The wicked person is trapped by the word of his own hands. Wicked people, all of the nations who forget God, will return to the grave. Needy people will not always be forgotten. Nor will the hope of oppressed people be lost forever. Arise, O Lord. Do not let mortals gain any power. Let the nations be judged in your presence. Strike them with the terror, O Lord. Let the nations know that they are only mortal."*

When the song was over, the crowd of believers shouted, "God is great, God is great."

Peter replied, God is great. Now. Peace be upon all of you, brothers and sisters."

Pye said to Peter, "God has truly blessed you."

"God has blessed you also, Pye," Peter replied. "God has blessed me and I can't thank him enough. Whenever I think about the Lord, it brings me so much Joy. I don't want to stop singing. I love the Lord my God with all of my heart."

"Thank you, Mr. Peter for singing for me," said Pearl.

"Come, Pearl," Pye said. "It's bedtime. Say good night."

Pearl said goodnight to everyone and gave Ann a big hug and told her she loved her.

One of the leaders of the travelers said, "The last two nights have been a blessing to us because of your singing. Before you came we were very sad, but because of your songs we are happy. Your singing has increased our faith. When we are glorifying the Lord in song it does something to the soul."

"Yes, it does," said Peter.

As they were walking to their tents three men approached them. One of them said, "We just arrived. Could you tell us where you brothers and sisters are going?"

"We are going to Galilee," Thomas said.

"That is where we just came from," he said.

"Do you have news of John the Baptist?" Thomas asked.

"John the Baptist?" another one of them said. "Why do you ask about him?"

"We are going to Galilee to ask King Herod to free him."

"Oh, are all the people here going to Galilee to ask King Herod to free John the Baptist?"

"Yes," said Thomas.

"So what news do you have about him?" Paul asked.

"We know nothing. We cannot help you." The three men departed.

Then one of the travelers came to them and said, "What

did those Pharisees want?"

"What Pharisees?" Thomas asked.

"Those three you were talking to. They are Pharisees."

"They wanted to know where we were going," Thomas answered.

The traveler then said, "I became worried when I saw them talking to you. Okay, goodnight brothers."

When they reached their tent, Peter said. "I hope we didn't say anything to the Pharisees that we shouldn't have said." The others agreed.

# Chapter 12

Two days later the three Pharisees were in Galilee. They stood in front of King Herod and reported, "My king, there are thousands of John's followers coming to Galilee to break him out of prison. We barely escaped with our lives. We rode all day and night to get here so you would have time to prepare for them."

King Herod said, "You will be well rewarded for your loyalty. Then Herod turned to one of his generals and said, "Prepare my army."

One of the Pharisees said, "If I may suggest something my king?"

"Speak," the king said.

"Thank you, my lord. We saw them and they are well armed. You may lose many soldiers in the battle, but if your soldiers attack them in their camp at night, while they are sleeping, you may not lose as many soldiers."

"That is a good idea," King Herod said. "I will double your reward."

"Thank you, my lord," the Pharisee said.

Back at the camp of the believers, right after the congregational prayer, Pearl asked Ann to sing her another song. Ann would not sing. Instead she offered to tell Pearl a story. Ann climbed on her donkey and placed Pearl on the donkey with her.

"I will tell you the story of Noah. Long ago, there lived

a man named Noah. Now Noah was a true believer in the One God. God knew Noah's heart and God was pleased with Noah. At that time the earth was full of evil people. God sent Noah to warn the people before a painful chastisement came upon them. Noah went to the people and said, 'O, my people, I have come to warn you that you must serve God and obey him. God will forgive you for your sins.' The people would not listen to Noah. Noah called out to God and said, 'Oh my Lord, surely I have called to my people by night and day. But my call has only made them worse."

"They were very bad people, weren't they?" Pearl said.

"Yes, they were," said Ann. Then she continued her story. "Noah tried to talk to them again. He said, 'Ask forgiveness from your Lord. Surely, He is most forgiving and all powerful. Do you not see how God has created the heavens, and made the moon a light for us, and made the sun a lamp for us?' But they still would not listen. Then Noah said, 'My Lord, surely they will not stop disobeying you. They want to do what they want to do and will not stop.' God said to Noah, 'I will destroy all of the evil people on the face of the earth. Make yourself a big ship out of wood and cover it with tar inside and outside."

"What is tar, Miss Ann?" Pearl asked.

"Tar is dark and sticky. It is the black stuff that they put on the roof of a house or building."

"I know what it is now," Pearl said. "It keeps the rain from coming into the house."

"Right," said Ann and continued the story. "When the people saw Noah building a ship they made fun of him. When the ship was finished, God told Noah to bring two of every living creature into the ship, male and female. He told Noah to go into the ship with his family because he was going to send down rain to the earth for forty days and forty nights. God said, 'I will destroy everything on the face of the earth.' So Noah and his family went into the ark as God commanded."

"Did the rain come like God said?" the little girl asked Ann.

Ann smiled and said, "Yes, seven days later the rain came, and it continued to rain for forty days. The water increased and lifted the ark up from the ground and the ark floated on top of the water. The water covered the highest mountains. After forty days the rain stopped. Noah and his family stayed on the ship for over one hundred and fifty days. Then God spoke to Noah. Noah came out of the ark as God had told him. God blessed Noah and his sons and said, 'Be fruitful and multiply and replenish the earth.' For the first time, God gave man permission to eat meat. God said to Noah, 'Do not eat meat with blood in it.' God also told Noah, 'I am going to make my promise to you and your descendants and every living thing on earth. I will never destroy the earth again with a flood. I will put my rainbow in the clouds to be a sign of my promise to the earth. And that is the story of Noah," said Ann.

"I liked that story, Miss Ann. I have seen a rainbow. They are so pretty," Pearl exclaimed.

"Yes, they are," said Ann.

"Thank you for telling me that story, Miss Ann," said Pearl.

"You are welcome, Pearl." After Ann finished her story she sent Pearl back to her mother.

# Chapter 13

Now on the hill overlooking the camp, was King Herod's army and with them were the three Pharisees. One of the Pharisees said, "It looks like they are sleeping. You should attack them now.

"Are you sure?" the general said.

"Yes," the Pharisee said.

The general replied, "If you are wrong you will pay with your life, Pharisee."

The battle cry was sounded and the soldiers charged down the hill to the camp. The believers heard the soldier's battle cry. They did not know what was happening. It was a very dark night. The moon was not out, and the only light was from the campfires. The soldiers were afraid because they couldn't see. They started killing anything that moved. The believers ran all around trying to save themselves.

Pye ran though the camp calling out to Pearl, but she could not find her. Pye began to cry but she didn't stop looking for the little girl. The soldiers killed men, women, and children.

Finally, the killing stopped and the soldiers left.

Ann and the others went looking for Pearl and her mother. They looked and looked but could not find them. Suddenly, Peter heard Pye screaming, and said to the others, "Look to your right. I hear Pye calling for Pearl.

Thomas shouted, "I see her!"

"Pye!" Ann shouted.

When Pye saw them, she started running and shouted for Peter. When she reached them she didn't see Pearl. Tears fell from her eyes and ran down her face. "Have you seen my baby?" she cried.

Tears began to fall from Ann and Peter's eyes, too.

"We have not seen Pearl," Ann said.

"We will find her," Peter said.

"Over here," Ann yelled after they had searched for hours.

Pye went over to where Ann was and started screaming, "My baby, my baby. She's dead. Oh my God. What have they done?"

Peter opened his arms and Pye ran into them. "God giveth and God taketh away. Pearl is with God now," he said.

"We are here for you, Pye," Ann said.

Paul picked Pearl's bloody body up from the ground and took her back to their tent. At dawn, they buried Pearl. Peter sang another song of David's.

After Peter finished singing, the people said, "We are going back home before we are killed too."

With a sad look on his face, Peter said, "What is wrong with you people? Are you believers in the power of the One God or not? We fear God and God alone. Don't listen to me. Listen to what the servant of God sung about being afraid of anything or anyone other than God. Peter began singing, "*The Lord is my light and my salvation. Who is there to fear? The Lord is my life's fortress. Who is there to be afraid of? Evildoers closed in on me to tear me to pieces. My opponents and enemies stumbled and fell. Even though an army sets up camp against me, my heart will not be* afraid. Even though a war breaks out against me, I will still have confidence in the Lord. I have asked one thing from the Lord. This I will seek; to remain in the Lord's house all the days of my life in order to gaze at the Lord's beauty and to search for an answer in His temple. He hides me in His shelter when there is trouble. He keeps me hidden in His tent. He sets me high on a rock. Now my head will be raised above my enemies who surround me. I will offer sacrifices with shouts of joy in His tent. I will sing and make music to praise the Lord. Hear, O Lord, when I cry aloud. Have pity on me, and answer me. When you said 'Seek My face,' my heart said to You, O Lord, I will seek your face. Do not hide your face from me. Do not angrily turn me away. You have been my help. Do not leave me. Do not abandon me, O God, my savior. Even if my father and mother abandon me, the Lord will take care of me. Teach me Your way, O Lord. Lead me on a level path because I have enemies who spy on me. Do not surrender me to the will of my opponents. False witnesses have risen against me. They breathe out violence. I believe that I will see the goodness of the Lord in this world of the living. Wait with hope for the Lord. Be strong and let your heart be courageous. Yes, wait with hope for the Lord."

Then the innkeeper shouted, "I will continue with you, Peter."

Other shouts rang out throughout the crowd, "I will go with you, Peter."

Tears ran down Peter's face. "God is great. God is great."

In Galilee the general was giving his report to King Herod. "My king, I don't understand it. We didn't lose any of our men, not one."

Immediately, one of the Pharisees said, "The gods were surely with us."

"Yes, you are right. It is a sign from the gods. Maybe the Baptist isn't a prophet of God after all. Were all of his followers killed?" the king asked.

"I do not know, it was very dark. But I do know that they will not come to Galilee," said the general.

"Good," said King Herod. "And thank you also," the king said to the Pharisees.

"Our job is to serve you, my king," one of the Pharisees said.

Then one of the Sadducees said, "My king, we really have much to celebrate tonight. Not only is it your birthday, but now we have a victory to celebrate also."

The king replied, "Yes, this is a happy time. Do not wait, let the celebration begin."

Back at the believers' camp, they prepared to leave for Galilee. Pye said, "I don't think that I will go to Galilee."

Ann replied, "It is not good for you to be alone right now."

Then Peter said, "Please, stay with us. We will be your family if you will let us." The others agreed.

Tears rolled down Pye's face. "I thank God for bringing you into my life. I will stay with you."

"We need you as much as you need us, thank you for staying with us," Peter said.

"Come on, the others are leaving," Thomas said, and they started their way.

In Galilee the celebration had started. King Herod had a wife. Her name was Herodias. She had a daughter. Herodias hated John the Baptist. Herodias told her daughter to dance for the king and his guests and she did. The king was mesmerized with her dancing. After she finished dancing, her mother said to the king, "What are you going to give my daughter for dancing for you and your guests?"

The king replied, "Anything that she wants in my kingdom."

Then Herodias called her daughter over to her and whispered into her ear.

Herodias' daughter said, "Did you say anything, my king?"

With a smile on his face, King Herod said, "Yes, anything, but do not ask for my throne." All of the king's guests laughed. "Name it," said the king.

"I want the head of John the Baptist on a golden platter."

The king and his guests laughed. Then the king said, "No, really, what do you want?"

She said again, "I want the head of John the Baptist on a golden platter."

"Are you crazy?" King Herod said.

"You promised my daughter anything she desired," Herodias said to the king,

The king said, "You are insane too!"

Herodias replied, "You are not going to break your promise in front of all of your guests, are you?"

Everyone looked at King Herod to see what he was going to do. With a sad look on his face, he ordered John the Baptist's head to be brought to him on a platter. One of the soldiers left to carry out the king's order and the celebration continued. A short time later, the soldier returned with a gold platter in his hands. John the Baptist's head was on it. When they saw it, there was silence. No one said or did anything. Since there was no noise in the banquet hall, everyone heard shouting coming from outside.

"Free John the Baptist...Free John the Baptist."

"Who is that?" the king asked.

One of the soldiers went to the window and looked out. He said, "There are thousands of people out there.

"Free John, free John, free John."

The king said, "Bring me their leader.

So, the general left with a hundred men. When the general and his soldiers reached the crowd, the believers were still shouting, "Free John."

The general commanded one of his soldiers to blow the horn. When he did, the crowd stopped shouting. "Who is your leader? I need to talk to him," the general shouted.

The crowd of believers shouted out, John the Baptist is our leader and your king has put him in prison."

The general then said, "Someone here is in charge."

One of the believers came up to the general and said, "My name is John also and these people have followed me here."

"Come with me," the general ordered John. The general took him before the king, "This is one of the leaders."

"Who are you?" the king asked.

"My name is John. I follow the teaching of John the Baptist. We have come from all over the land to ask you for his freedom."

"If my army had not killed your warriors last night, you and the rest of your people would be at my gate trying to break him out," King Herod said. "I want you to know that nothing happens in my kingdom that I don't know about."

John said, "I don't know what you have been told about last night, but let me tell you the truth. We had no warriors with us last night. The only ones your soldiers killed were helpless men, women, and children. Look out of your window. Do you see any warriors or weapons?"

"No," the king replied.

"If it was day time instead of darkness last night your soldiers would have seen only unarmed men and women. We only came to ask you to show mercy on your birthday. Will you free John the Baptist?"

The king replied, "May the One God forgive me. I have killed his prophet."

"What?" John said.

Then Herodias said, "Yes, John the Baptist is dead, and he was no prophet of any gods. He was only a troublemaker, and we are glad that he is dead."

"Close your mouth," the king said to her. "Bring me those three Pharisees. Now!" he ordered.

"May we have his body?" John asked.

"Yes," King Herod replied.

"May I go now?" John asked. The king gave John permission to leave, so he left with the prophet's body.

When the three Pharisees stood before the king, King Herod said, "You have lied to me."

One of the Pharisees spoke up, "My king, we only wanted to protect you and our queen."

The king replied, "You are lying. You and the rest of your band of so called holy men were only trying to protect yourselves. I should have you three beheaded."

"Please, please, I beg you. Don't kill us my king," one of them pleaded.

King Herod said, "I will not kill you. You will go to the east wing in three different rooms. You will stay there for five years and pray for my forgiveness."

"Thank you," said the Pharisees.

"Out of my sight," ordered the king.

John returned to the believers carrying a bloody sack. "They have killed him," he told the believers.

The believers said, "God is great. John the Baptist is with God now. God is great."

"I would not want to be Herod for all the gold in the world," Peter said.

"Or anyone who had anything to do with this death," Thomas said. "They will pay for what they have done."

At John the Baptist's burial the people asked Peter to say a few words and to sing a song.

Peter replied, "I was not a follower of John the Baptist, and I know very little about him. What shall I say?"

An old man said, "God will give you the words, Peter."

"Thank you," said Peter. Then Peter went in front of the people and said, "We know that John the Baptist was a prophet of the One God. John's reward for being upright is being with God. This is the greatest reward that one could hope for. Do not worry. God will repay them for killing His servant. God is the greatest. I will try to tell you the best I can what God has said in the Holy Scriptures.

"For no reason will God leave the believers in the condition you are in. Be patient until God separates the evil from the good. God chooses whom He pleases. Believe in God and His prophets. If you believe, guard yourself against evil. Then you shall have a great reward. God is aware of what you do. He has surely heard the saying of those who said, 'God is poor and we are rich.' God will record what they said. God will say, 'Taste the chastisement of the burning. This is for what your own hands have sent before you.' Now God is not in the least unjust to His servants. I ask God's forgiveness if I have changed His message to you. If you heard anything confusing or wrong, it came from me. But if you heard anything good, it came from God. I remember a song my father would sing to me that David sang. David had many songs to praise the One God. This song I feel is appropriate for this time because we know that three wicked men have lied on us. We ask for help for the only one who can help us. That one is God Almighty."

Peter began to sing. *"Open your ears to my words, O Lord. Consider my innermost thoughts. Pay attention to my cry for help, my King and my God, because I pray only to you. In the morning, O Lord, hear my voice, and I wait. You are not a God who takes pleasure in wickedness. Evil will never be your guest. Those who brag cannot stand in your sight. You hate all troublemakers. You destroy those who tell lies. The Lord is disgusted with bloodthirsty and deceitful people. But I will enter your house because of your great mercy. Out of reverence for you, I will bow toward your Holy temple. O Lord, lead me in your righteousness because of those who spy on me. Make your way in front of me smooth. Nothing in their mouths is truthful. Destructions come from their hearts. Their throats are open graves. They flatter with their tongues. Condemn them, O God. Let their own schemes be their downfall. Throw them out for their many crimes because they have rebelled against you. But let all who take refuge in you rejoice. Let them sing with joy forever. Protect them, and let those who love your name triumph in you. You bless righteous people, O Lord, like a large shield. You surround them with your favor."*

After Peter finished singing, he said, "We are believers in the God of Abraham and so was John the Baptist. We know that all things work for the good of God."

Then all the believers chanted, "God is great, God is great."

"Where to now, Peter?" Thomas asked.

Peter answered, "Maybe Jesus is still in Jericho, but if not, someone will know where he went."

"You know being a believer is hard work," Paul said.

"Yes, it is," Pye agreed. "But the harder you work to please God, the bigger your reward shall be."

"We should be on our way," said Paul.

The others agreed. "Are you all right, Pye?" Peter asked.

"I am good, thank God," she answered.

"That makes me happy," Peter said.

Pye had a sad look on her face, but Peter could not see it. Ann did and she said, Pye come walk with me for a while. So they left.

# Chapter 14

With tears falling from her eyes, Pye said, "I miss my baby. I remember when she was born and my husband saying how lovely she was. That he couldn't believe through us how God had given life to such a precious one."

"I am sorry, Pye. I know you are in pain. I can see it all over your face, especially in your eyes," Ann said, fighting back tears of her own." That was beautiful what your husband said about precious and sweet little Pearl."

"Yes it was," Pye agreed. "If he could have, I believe he would have sang it, but he couldn't even carry one note, much less an entire song. Peter reminds me in some ways of my late husband."

"I wonder what Peter will say when his first child is born," Ann said.

"I don't know him that well, but if I had to guess I would say he would sing the baby a song," Pye replied, smiling.

"You know, I think you're right," Ann agreed. "What did you mean when you said Peter reminds you of your husband?"

"I can't put my finger on it but it's something about him. I can't wait to see Jesus. I pray that Jesus can ask God to give Peter his sight," Pye replied.

"You like Peter?" Ann asked.

"Yes, I like him very much."

"Well, you don't have anyone and Peter doesn't have anyone," Ann said.

"Peter doesn't like me like that," Pye said.

"But do you like him in that way?" Ann asked

"Everyone I seem to love dies. I fear loving anyone again."

"Pye you cannot be afraid to love or be loved." Pye didn't respond. "Love is all we have. That's what makes us happy. Do you still love God?"

"Yes, I still love God. I always will."

"Then you have been lying to yourself. God has not died, so that means everyone you have loved has not died," Ann said.

"You are right, but Peter has never been married. He is probably looking forward to marrying a virgin. No one will marry me now because I have been married and have had a child."

"Don't be so hard on yourself. It was God's will that you had a child and that you were married. It is also God's will that you are alone now. So, thank God for the happiness you have had and thank God for the happiness that you *will* have, Pye."

"I do thank God for you and the others. No matter what happens between me and Peter I will always love you all."

"We are here for you," Ann said.

"It's almost time to make camp. I will cook," said Pye.

An hour later they all stopped to make camp. Pye started cooking and Ann volunteered to help her. Ann suggested that Thomas and Paul start a fire and go get some water from the river. Thomas agreed to go and get the water, so Paul started gathering wood to make the fire.

"What can I do?" Peter asked.

"You can help me cut up the vegetables if you want," Pye said.

"Okay," Peter replied. "This has been some kind of year."

"This year is almost over. Maybe next year will be better for you, Peter," Pye replied.

"I didn't mean that this year had been a bad year," Peter replied. "I just meant that so many things have happened. I have never had a year like this before."

"I know what you mean, this year has tested my faith also," Pye replied.

"Yes," said Peter. "Faith is tested in many ways. Like believing that if God puts something on your mind to do that you have never done before. Some people will say to themselves, I can't do it. All true believers know that God teaches man what we know not. God will never tell you to do something and not help you. That's how you will know if God told you to do it. You will be able to do things that you could not do before."

Pye then said, "You are a true believer. Anyone who is around you their faith will become stronger."

"You see, we all know that life's journey will end with death. I try to enjoy the journey through this life and pray that when the journey is over, I will be with God."

"Do you want children?" Pye asked Peter.

"Yes, I would like to have children one day," said Peter. When I find Jesus and God gives me my sight."

"What if you don't get your sight back?" Pye asked. "Does that mean that you will not marry and have children?"

"What kind of father or husband could I be not being able to see?"

"Peter, you see everything with your heart and that's better than seeing with your eyes. You would make a very good father and husband, whether you receive sight or not."

"I do want a wife and children very much," Peter admitted.

"Are you two finished with the vegetables?" Ann asked.

After Ann and Pye were done cooking, Ann said, "Peter, would you like me to fix your food?"

"No," Pye said. "I will fix his plate. That is, if it's okay with you, Peter."

"Yes, thank you," said Peter.

"Who wants to fix my plate?" Thomas asked, laughing.

"Yes, who will fix my plate?" Paul followed. "When he didn't get a response, Paul said, "I guess we'll fix our own plates."

"I will fix plates for you," Pye replied.

"We were just joking," Paul said.

"I don't mind," Pye said.

Then Peter said, "I will fix their plates." They all laughed.

While they were eating, Paul said, "I miss my wife."

"Does that mean you're ready to go home?" Thomas asked.

"Thomas, why are you talking to Paul like that?" Peter asked.

"He acts like he is the only one that has someone waiting for him."

"That's not what he said," Peter answered. "He only said that he misses his wife. What is really bothering you?"

"Forgive me, Paul," Thomas said. "I miss Hope very much also and when you said that it made me think about her."

"When we left home we didn't think that we would be gone this long. I will understand if you brothers want to go home," Peter said.

"Why are we on this journey?" Pye asked. "I would bet

every one of us is here because of love."

Paul said, "Thomas and I didn't come for love, we only came to help Peter find Jesus."

"Why are you here, Ann?" Pye asked.

"I really don't know, it just happened."

"You see, I know the only reason I came with you is because you showed me love. So love is the reason for me being here. Paul, you said that the reason you and Thomas are here is to help Peter. And you, Ann, you said that you don't know why you're here. Well, let me tell you all something. Love comes in many ways. Like the love we have for our father and mother, our brother and sister or the love we have for our spouse and children. But the most important love of all is the love we have for God." Pye continued talking, "Paul, you and Thomas are here because the both of you love Peter like a brother. And for you, Ann, you love to help people. God loves those who help their neighbor."

Peter said, "Jesus is always talking about loving your neighbor. He even said you should love your enemies."

Thomas then said, "What do you mean love your enemies?"

Peter answered, "Jesus said, 'Love your enemies, be kind to those who hate you, bless those who curse you, pray for those who insult you. If someone takes your coat, don't stop him from taking your shirt. Give to everyone who asks you for something. If someone takes what is yours, don't insist on getting it back. Do for other people everything you want them to do for you. If you love those who love you, do you deserve any thanks for that? Sinners do that too. If you lend anything to those from whom you expect to get something back, do you deserve any thanks for that? Sinners also lend to sinners to get back what they lend. Rather, love your enemies, help them, and lend to them without expecting to get anything back. Then you will have a great reward.'"

"I understood everything you said, except when you talked about lending. I thought the word lend meant to give and get back," said Paul.

"Yes, you are right, but the word lend has more than one meaning. One of the meanings for lend is *to give*. You see, when Jesus was talking to the true believers about how to treat their brothers and sisters—"

Pye interrupted Peter. "We are all brothers and sisters because we came from Adam and Eve."

"You are right in a way," Peter said, "but, I look at it like this. This generation is the generation of Noah. All believers who believe in the One God are brothers and sisters. But those who don't believe in the One God are our cousins. I believe that is what Jesus is trying to make us understand. You see, to be someone's brother or sister you must have the same mother or father. That's why Jesus is always telling the true believers about their heavenly father."

"When I heard Jesus talking to the believers, he said, 'your Heavenly Father, our Father,'" Ann said.

"You have met Jesus?" Pye asked.

"Yes, I have met Jesus, but I didn't get to touch him. I will never forget his voice or how he looked."

"I feel a little tired, I think it's time for me to go to sleep," said Thomas. Paul and Ann agreed with him.

"I think I will stay up a little longer," Peter said.

"So will I," Pye said. The others said goodnight to them and left.

"Do you have any other songs other than King David's?"

Pye asked Peter.

"Yes, I have a few that I have written," he answered. "I just started on a new song."

"What is the name of it, and what is it about?"

"I haven't thought of a name for it yet, but it's a love song. It's about a woman telling her man how much she loves him and how she will help him to become a better man. She tells him her love will make him strong. Then she says 'You will be able to count on my love forever more. That's all I have so far."

"That's beautiful, Peter."

"Thank you. I have a lot more work to do on it."

"Peter, when this trip is over what are you going to do?"

"I would like to go all over the land and see as much as I can see."

"Have you thought about what you will do if you don't get your sight back?" she asked.

"I don't think about not getting my sight," Peter replied. "God will give me sight if it will bring me closer to him. You see, I pray that if sight will take me further from God, then do not give me my sight. I would rather stay a blind believer, than to become a seeing disbeliever. So, no matter what happens, I will be happy, because if God gives me sight I will know that I will be closer to him, and if he doesn't give me my sight I will still be happy knowing that God has kept me on the straight path."

"You have a godly way of looking at things. That's what makes you special."

There's nothing special about the way I look at things. All true believers try to put God first in everything they do and say and most of all what they think. Because a true believer knows when they put God first everything turns out okay. The true believer knows that God is the only one who always has their best interest at heart. I like me, because I do and say things that are not in my best interest."

"I hope what I say is not unladylike, but here goes. It's so easy for any woman to love you. When a woman sees and hears the godly things you do and say that is what they fall in love with. Every woman wants a man who loves and fears God, if she's in her right mind."

"I don't know what to say," Peter said.

"You don't have to say anything. I think that I should go to bed now," Pye answered.

"I enjoy talking to you very much," Peter said. I have a problem talking to women, but with you, I don't know. It's something about you that's different.

"It makes me happy that you are comfortable talking to me. It's getting late, I'm going to bed now. Goodnight, Peter."

Moments later, Peter went into his tent. Paul and Thomas were still awake.

"I need someone to talk to," Peter said.

"Didn't you just finish talking to Pye?" Thomas asked.

"That's what I want to talk about."

"What's going on?" Paul asked.

"I think she just told me that she loves me."

"What!" Paul said.

"Yes," said Peter. "I think she said that she loves me."

"What exactly did she say?" Thomas asked.

"She said that women love men who love and fear God, and that I am a man who loves and fears God."

"I think you're right," Paul said. "She's in love with you. So what are you going to do?"

"I don't know," Peter replied.

"If I were you, I would talk to Ann about it," Paul said.

"That's a good idea," Peter agreed.

Early the next morning, Peter left his tent. Ann was preparing to cook. She greeted him.

"How are you this morning?" Ann asked.

"Puzzled," Peter replied.

"What are you puzzled about?"

"It's about Pye. I don't know how to tell her that I don't want to get married right now without hurting her feelings. She just lost her daughter. I know she needs someone."

"Yes, you are right. Pye is reaching out for someone to call her own," Ann said.

"I think she is a good woman, but when I get married I want to be able to concentrate totally on my wife. Right now, the only thing on my mind is finding Jesus."

"I understand, Peter, and so will Pye. Tell her what you just told me," Ann replied.

"But what if..."

"Good morning, Pye," Ann said, cutting Peter off so he wouldn't say anything else about Pye.

"Good morning, to both of you," Pye replied. "How are you feeling this morning, Peter?

"Fine," he replied.

"Are you hungry, Peter?" Pye asked.

"I was just about to fix breakfast," Ann said.

"That's okay, I will fix it," Pye said. "Come talk to me while I cook, Peter."

"I was talking to Ann," he replied.

"No, go on," said Ann. "We can talk later." Ann walked away, leaving the two of them alone to talk.

Pye said to Peter, "Have you thought about what we

talked about last night?"

"Yes, I have," Peter said. "You're very nice and I look at you as a good friend and I hope you think of me as your friend also."

"Peter."

"Wait, Pye. Let me finish. Maybe after we find Jesus we can think about other things, but for right now the only thing on my mind is finding Jesus. I hope you understand."

"I know how important it is to you that you find Jesus, and I want to help you find him. Don't worry, we will always be friends."

"Maybe we will become more than friends in time, if it's God will," Peter said.

"Yes, if it's God will," Pye repeated.

Pye started fixing breakfast and Ann returned to help her. Peter and Thomas decided to go and wake Paul. After they woke him up, they told him Ann and Pye were preparing the food. They sat around talking until Ann informed them that the food was ready.

While they were sitting around talking, a party of men came into the camp.

"Peace be upon you, brothers and sisters," said one of the men.

"Peace be upon you also," Peter said. "Come sit down and have some food."

"No, thank you, brother. We don't have time. We are looking for a man eater. He has killed five people in my village. We have been hunting him for three days now."

"Where is your village?" Paul asked.

"It's about three or four hours away from here," one of the men said.

"Where did you last see signs of him?" Peter asked.

"We lost his tracks two days ago."

"Come, let's go back to your village," Paul said.

"No," the man said. "We must find him."

"If he has killed five in your village, he will come back," Paul said.

The men agreed to return to their village with Paul. When Ann and Pye asked what was going on, Peter said to them, "Paul is going to kill the lion for them."

"Paul is going to kill a lion?" Ann asked, amazed.

"Yes, he is going to kill the lion for them," Peter answered. "Paul is the best hunter and the most feared warrior of our village."

"Paul is so quiet. I would have never guessed that about him." Ann said.

"One of the reasons Paul came with me is to protect me," Peter said.

"Let's get our stuff together," Paul said. A few minutes later they were headed towards the village. While they were walking, Paul said to Peter, "Forgive me for not asking whether you wanted to go or not."

"There was no need to ask me. You know what my answer would have been. They need your help and God brought them to our camp for you to help them," Peter said.

"I thank God for you, Peter. You have always helped me with keeping God in everything that I do."

Peter said, "I must have patience. I will find Jesus when God is ready for me to find him. You know Paul, you have always protected me even when we were children. You always kept the other kids from hurting me or picking on me. Thank you for that."

"I never said it before, but you are my brother, Peter. We

don't have the same worldly father or mother but we have something better. We have the same heavenly father."

"Paul, look over here," one of the men said. Paul went over to the man and the man pointed to the ground. There were lion tracks.

"How much further is your village?" Paul asked.

"Just over the hill," the man replied.

When they reached the village all they could hear was crying. "They killed my babies," a woman cried out.

One of the men from the Village ran up to them and said, "There are three of them."

"Three?" Peter said. "Paul, what are you going to do?"

Paul instructed the men to gather all the young men together so that he could talk to them. Once the young men had gathered, Paul began talking to them.

When the leader of the village returned, he saw Paul speaking to the men. "Who is this man that has called my men together?" he asked.

One of the men from the village replied, "I called the men together."

"And who is he?" the leader asked, pointing at Paul.

"We met him when we were hunting the lion. He offered to kill the lion for us," the man replied.

Becoming upset, the leader said, "I didn't ask you where you met him, I asked you who he is."

When Paul heard his words, he said to the leader, "My name is Paul. I believe in the God of Abraham."

Then the leader said, my name is Job, and I also believe in the One God."

"I know," said Paul. "Don't be angry with this young man for I asked him to gather the men together."

The leader then said, "Ham, come here."

"Yes, Father," the young man replied.

Job said to Paul, "This is my son. Welcome to our village."

Paul introduced the others with him to Job. He then told him that after God sent his son into their camp he decided to come and help them with their problem.

"I thank God for you, my brother," Job said. "We have no knowledge on how to hunt a man eater. I believe you do or you would not have come."

"Yes, I can kill them for you with God's help," Paul said.

"What do you want us to do, my brother?" asked Job.

Paul answered, "I need all of the young men together with drums."

Job instructed the men to gather drums. He asked Paul, "Where were you and your friends going?"

"We are looking for Jesus," Paul answered. "My friend, Peter, believes if he finds Jesus, God will give Jesus the power to give him his sight."

Job said, "God has given many people what they wanted through Jesus."

"Yes, I know," said Paul.

The young man returned with the drums and asked Paul what they should do next. Paul said, "We must find the man-eaters and separate them. I must warn you, it will not be easy."

Peter said, "Let's pray before you brothers go out." He led them in prayer saying, "Oh my God, it is written for the true believers. Therefore, let those fight in the way of God. Those who sacrifice this worldly life for the hereafter and whoever fights in the way of God then be he slain or be he victorious, God shall grant him a mighty reward. Those who believe fight in the way of God, and those who disbelieve fight in the way of the devil. Fight therefore against the friends of the devil. Surely the friends of the devil are weak. These lions are evil, so go fight against the evil ones in the way of God. And fear not because we are the believers in the Word of God. God is great, God is great, God is great."

All of the men repeated, 'God is great' and then they left.

The men had been gone for about two hours when one of them shouted, "Over here, over here."

Paul and Job ran over and Job said to Paul, "It looks like we found two of them."

Paul bent down and looked at the footprints and said, "No, it is all three of them.

"How much further ahead of us are they?" Job asked.

"About an hour," Paul answered. Then Paul called the men together and said, "We will soon come upon the lions. They can sense fear, so remember to fear not for God is with us."

A little more than an hour had passed when Paul spotted the lions. He instructed the men to start beating the drums. Each man with a drum had two or three men alongside him with spears.

"We must drive them out into the open," said Paul.

"They are splitting up," Ham said.

"Don't let them!" Paul shouted.

The lions charged toward the men. To Paul's surprise, the men with the drums started charging toward the lions. The lions then turned and ran the other way. The lions ran right into the men with the spears. The men killed all three of them. Then they shouted, "God is great, God is great."

Job looked at Paul and said, "God is great."

"Yes, He is," Paul replied.

Ham ran up to Job. "Father, father, did you see that?"

"I did, my son," said Job. "Let's go home." When they reached the village, they were still praising God in song. The others heard them singing and ran out to meet them singing the same song. In the front were six men carrying the three lions.

Peter said to Thomas, "What's happening?"

Thomas answered, "Paul is back and he's killed the lions."

"All three?" Peter asked.

"Yes, all three," Thomas said.

Job said to the people, "We will have a burnt offering to the Lord for giving us the victory over the evil ones." Then Job turned to Paul and said, "After the offering you and your friends must come to my house for the banquet."

"Thank you so much for inviting us to the banquet, but we must be going," said Paul.

"You and your friends must come," said Job.

Peter then said, "We will come."

The others smiled and said, "We will be happy to come."

At the feast Job sat Paul and the others at the head of the table with him. They ate and talked about God's mercy. Once the feast was over, Job invited them to stay with him for the night. They accepted Job's invitation.

Job said to Ham, "Take them to their rooms."

Peter and the others thanked Job, and Ham took them to their rooms. Ann and Pye were talking when Ann said to Pye, "I had a joyful time at the feast."

"I did too," Pye said. "Did you notice that Peter didn't drink any wine."

"No, I didn't," Ann replied. "Come to think about it, I have never seen Peter drink wine. I wonder why?"

Down the hall, in the men's room, they were also

talking. Paul said to Peter and Thomas, "I wish you were there today to witness faith in action. Those brothers are true believers. When the lions turned on them, they had no fear because of God's word. They ran right at the man-eaters. And I'm not talking about the men with the spears. I mean the men with the drums were the first to charge the lions. I have never seen anything like it."

"Most people wouldn't understand anyone like that," Peter said. "They would call them crazy or religious fanatics. But a true believer understands, because a true believer knows when they are doing the best that they can do with the knowledge of what God wants them to do, then they have no need to fear anything. Not even dying. A true believer is not crazy or a religious fanatic. A true believer does not want to die, but we don't know what we will be doing tomorrow, so it may be better for us to die today as a true believer than to live until tomorrow and become a disbeliever. A true believer is fearless for that reason. There will come a day when an army of true believers will fight in the way of God. Then the world will know that the God of Abraham still lives."

# Chapter 15

"Will Jesus be in Galilee when we get there?" Pye asked as they continued their journey.

"I hope so," said Peter.

Just then they saw a woman sitting alone on a large rock. She was very pretty. "Peace be upon you my sister," said Ann.

"What is that smell?" Thomas asked the woman.

"It's beef stew," she replied. "Come have some."

Thomas smiled and said, "Thank you, but it's too many of us. Thank you anyway."

"Nonsense," she replied. "I have a big pot of stew. There is more than enough for all of us."

The smile never left Thomas face and he said, "Thank you. We would love to join you for some stew."

"You're welcome. Come on let's eat," she said.

Thomas went to the others and said, "Come on, we have been invited to eat." So they all stopped to eat.

She invited them to sit. Then Pye asked, "What is your name?"

"My name is Nadine," she replied.

"The stew is very good, Nadine," Peter said.

The others agreed and each told Nadine their names. Paul put his hand on Peter's shoulder and said, "Nadine has a very pretty smile."

Peter replied, "If her smile is half as good as her stew, her smile is not pretty, it's beautiful."

Smiling, Nadine said, "Where are you brothers and sisters going?"

Peter answered, "We are going to Galilee to see the man called Jesus. You are welcome to come with us if you want."

"I don't know, let me think about it," Nadine said.

After they finished eating, Peter asked, "Nadine, have you decided whether you are going with us to Galilee?"

She replied, "I would like to, but I can't."

"If you want to go, why can't you?" Peter asked.

"I have no money,' she replied.

"Don't worry about money," Peter said. "I have enough money for the both of us. I know how it is not to have money. There have been times in my life when I didn't have enough money to do any of the things I needed to do. I only had enough to eat. It made me feel so bad. Even though I didn't choose this for my life, it still makes me sad sometimes. When I remember that God is in control of all things, I thank God because it could be worse. You see, I know that everything God does or let's happen he has a reason. We might not know the reason that God is taking us through these changes, but that is where faith in God comes in. A true believer believes that God knows what's best."

"I know what you are saying is true, but sometimes I feel like giving up. Things are so hard for me right now," Nadine said.

Peter took her hand into his and said, "Hold on to the rope of God. Things in your life will get better. Just give it time. God has already worked out everything in your life. It's always darkest before the dawn, so just give it time."

"Thank you," Nadine said.

131

"You're welcome," said Peter.

"I would love to go with you," Nadine said.

They all departed. The women started talking about men. Ann said, "Men are our protectors."

"They are good for more than just protecting us," Pye said. "I use them for everything. What about you, Nadine. What do you use men for?"

"I don't use men," Nadine said humbly.

"All women use men in one way or another," Pye said.

"Some women are different," Nadine replied.

"Right, I heard you and Peter talking," said Pye.

"What are you trying to say?" Nadine asked.

"You know what I mean. Some women marry for money," Pye said.

"I would never marry for money," Nadine said. "I want a man who I can talk to and laugh with, someone to raise a family with. Most of all, someone I can trust. Money doesn't matter to me, God takes care of me.

"There are still some women who marry just for love," Ann said.

"That's crazy," Pye said.

"What are you women talking about?" Peter asked.

"Men," Ann replied.

Thomas and Paul were walking in front of them. Thomas said to Paul, "Nadine is so pretty."

"Yes, she is," Paul replied. Changing the subject, Paul said, "Galilee is just over those mountains."

Finally, they arrived in Galilee. It was a big city. Peter was so happy and it could be seen all over his face.

"What does it look like?" Peter asked.

"There are so many people," Nadine replied.

Peter told Paul to ask someone where they could find

Jesus. Paul went up to a man and said, "My brother, can you tell me where I can find the man they called Jesus?"

"He was here but he has left," the man answered.

"Where did he go?" Peter asked the man.

"I don't know," the man replied.

With the man's response, a very sad look appeared on Peter's face. Paul turned to Peter and said, "We will find him."

"God willing, we will," Peter replied.

"Where are we going to look now?" Thomas asked.

"All we have to do is find out which way he went," Paul said.

Pye saw a woman walking by and asked, "Do you know which way the man called Jesus went?"

"He went south," she said." I don't know what village he was going to, but I do know he went south."

"Thank you so very much," Pye said.

"You're welcome," the woman said.

"Do you think Peter will ever find Jesus?" Pye asked Ann as the women trailed a few feet behind the men.

"Only God knows," Ann replied.

"I pray that he does," Nadine said.

Peter said to Paul and Thomas, "I believe Nadine will be a big help to us."

"I guess so," said Thomas.

Then Paul said to Peter. "We have been gone for a long time."

"I know," said Peter. "We can go back home if you want to."

"We will give it a few more weeks," Paul said.

"Thank you, my brother," said Peter, "If we don't find Jesus in three weeks, we will return home."

"Don't I have a say in this?" Thomas asked.

"What do you want to do?" asked Peter.

"I want to go fishing," Thomas replied.

Peter and Paul laughed. "Okay, tomorrow we will go fishing," Peter said.

"I was just playing," Thomas said.

They traveled until they found a place to camp for the night.

The following morning after they finished eating, Peter said, "We are going east."

"But Jesus went south," Paul said.

"I know," said Peter.

"So why are we going east?" Paul asked.

Peter replied, "We're going fishing."

They all started walking east. Peter and Nadine were walking together.

Days went by, and Nadine never left Peter's side. The more they talked, the more Peter knew he loved Nadine. He had fallen in love. For the first time in his life, he felt someone understood him and her voice was so sweet to Peter's heart. There was just something about her voice. Every time she opened her mouth, a smile came on Peter's face. No matter how bad or sad he felt, when he heard Nadine's voice, he was okay. Peter loved Nadine like no other man had ever loved a woman before. They could talk about anything. Days went by like hours. Before they knew it, they were in a small village. They didn't know what village they were in. When Peter heard the people from the village talking, he asked Nadine where they were.

"I don't know," Nadine replied.

He then asked the others if they knew where they were. "I don't know where we are, but it looks like a nice village,"

Thomas said.

"I will ask someone where we are," Paul said. So Paul walked up to a young man and said, "Peace be upon you."

"Peace be upon you, my brother," the young man replied.

"Can you tell me the name of this village?" Paul asked.

"This is Nain," the young man answered.

"Oh, is the ocean near?" Paul asked.

"It's a little ways off but not that far," the young man replied.

"Thank you again," Thomas said. Then he said to the others, "Let's stay here for the night and tomorrow we can head south."

"What about going fishing?" Peter asked.

"We can go fishing any time. Let's find Jesus first," Thomas said.

They made camp. It had become late and everyone was asleep, except for Peter and Nadine. Peter was sitting up when Nadine walked by. She saw Peter sitting up so she called his name.

"Yes, Nadine," Peter replied.

"Would you like to walk down to the stream with me?"

"What stream?" Peter asked.

"One of the women told me about a stream where they wash," Nadine said.

"I would love to go with you," Peter said with a big smile on his face.

They walked to the stream hand in hand. "Let's stop here," Nadine said.

It was a beautiful night. God's night light was on, the moon was full. It lit up the night. Peter then asked, "Is that a waterfall I hear?"

"Yes," Nadine answered.

"Could you describe it to me?"

"No one could describe something so beautiful."

Peter smiled and said, "I know what you are saying. God's work is sometimes too beautiful for words. Do the best you can."

"The moon is full and the stars are shining so bright. Looking into the stream, it looks like two moons and many stars. With the sound of the waterfall in my ears and seeing all of this, it takes my breath away."

Peter then said, "One day we will see it together, God willing."

"What are you saying, Peter?" Nadine asked.

"I love you," Peter said. "I want to live the rest of my life with you."

"We have different ways of life," Nadine said. "It will not work."

"I didn't put these feelings in my heart, God did," Peter said. "I just want you to know how I feel about you. It's up to God now."

"I understand what you are saying and I love talking to you and being with you. But you see, loving someone and being in love with someone are two different things," said Nadine.

"Thank you for being honest with me," said Peter. "That's one of the things I love about you. I've been around many women, but I have never felt this way before about any woman. I know you're telling me that you don't want to marry me. You just want to be friends."

"I don't want to hurt you," said Nadine.

"I know you don't," Peter said and smiled. "I didn't tell you that I love you hoping that you would say you love me too. I told you to let you know how I feel about you. It would be nice if you were in love with me. You see, I know how I feel about a person the first time I meet them. I can imagine you're thinking, this man is crazy. Some people have called me crazy because I told them that my life is not complete without a wife. I believe God says a man needs a help mate. I feel that I have known you for a very long time. I know what I say might not make sense. Sometimes when you're in love, what you think, feel, and say doesn't make sense. I don't know if you will believe me or not, but you are the first woman that I feel loves me just for me. I feel it deep in my heart. I will love you until the end of time, and God knows that you are my one and only love."

"I have never known a man like you before," Nadine said. "You're a man who is unafraid to express his feelings. Usually men don't show their feelings, let alone talk about them. You're a very special person. I have only been around you a short time and I have strong feelings for you. Maybe in time I will fall in love with you. I like the feeling I get when we are together."

"Your words have given me hope and that makes me so very happy," Peter said.

"I think we should head back," said Nadine.

"Can we stay just a little while longer please," said Peter.

"Okay," Nadine replied. They stayed for about an hour, then they went back to camp. Nadine kissed Peter on the cheek and said goodnight.

"This has been one of the best nights of my life. Thank you. Goodnight, Nadine," Peter said with a smile on his face.

"Mine too," Nadine replied. They went to their individual tents and fell asleep.

The following morning, they all got up and had prayer together. After they finished praying, Peter asked the others if they were ready to leave. As usual Thomas asked if they could eat first. Peter agreed, so the women started to cook. Once the food was ready Pye called the brothers to come eat.

Everyone was eating when Pye looked at Nadine with an evil expression. She then turned to Peter and said, "Peter, did you sleep well last night?"

"Yes, I did, thank you for asking," Peter replied.

Ann looked at Nadine and smiled. Paul suggested they prepare to leave. Ten minutes later they were on their way.

Nadine went over to Pye and said, "I had no idea you liked Peter, please forgive me."

With her eyes full of water, fighting back tears, Pye replied, "No. Please forgive me. I had no right to act that way toward you. Peter has made it clear that he wants us to be nothing more than friends."

"I don't want to start any trouble between you and Peter or between you and me," Nadine said.

"You are not coming between anyone," Pye replied. "Nadine, you are such a nice person. Can you ever forgive me?"

"Yes, I forgive you," Nadine said. "I hope we can become friends."

"You have already proved that you are my friend and from this day forward, I will prove that I can be a friend to you also. I will become the best friend you have ever had. This, I promise."

Nadine smiled and said, "Thank you," and the two women hugged.

The brothers were also talking. Thomas was telling Paul

how cool it was to have two women fighting over you.

"Don't say that," Peter said to Thomas. "I didn't mean to hurt Pye, but God has shown me love in Nadine. I know now why I did not feel the same about Pye as she felt about me."

Paul said. "It will work itself out."

Thomas said, "We have not found Jesus, but we all have found love on this trip.

"You are right and that's the way of life. You start out looking for one thing and you find so many other things along the way. That's our trip throughout life," Peter said.

"You're right," Paul replied. "How many times have I started looking for something that I lost, and found something else I couldn't find?

# Chapter 16

"Perhaps Jesus went to Cana," said Paul.

"Okay, let's go to Cana first," Peter replied.

It took them a few days to get to Cana. Nadine was always by Peter's side. They talked and talked. Then Peter said, "Nay, you must forgive me."

"For what?" Nadine asked.

"I didn't mean to lie to anyone," Peter answered.

"What are you talking about?" Nadine asked.

Peter dropped his head and said, "I told you that I didn't know that Pye had feelings for me, but that is not true, but once I heard your voice I forgot everything. From the first time I heard you speak, I couldn't believe that sound could be so sweet. From that time on, I hear your voice with each beat of my heart. All I think about is holding you in my arms. I even stopped thinking about finding Jesus for a time. That's how much you mean to me. If I have to choose between you and my sight, I would choose you."

"I believe you, Peter," Nadine said. "I feel myself falling in love with you. We will find Jesus and God will give you your sight."

Peter reached out his hand and Nadine took his hand into hers. Then he slowly pulled her hand to his face and kissed it.

"I will never leave your side," said Nadine. She took her other arm and put it around Peter's neck.

He pulled Nadine close, their bodies were as one, and he whispered in her ear, "I was made to love you."

The group arrived in Cana. Paul said, "We're here. I see two pyramids with smoke coming out of the top."

Before they could reach the city gate, a sweet smell met them.

Peter said, I have never been to any place that smells this good."

"It does smell good," Nadine replied. "I wonder what kind of incense they are burning."

"Tell me what the village looks like," Peter said to Nadine.

"I'll tell you," Thomas said.

"No, let me," Nadine said.

"Okay." Thomas looked at Nadine with a smile on his face.

Nadine started telling Peter how the village looked. "It's a village but it's built like a city. It has a wall around it. The wall is about thirty feet tall but there is no gate."

"What kind of village is this?" Peter asked.

"A beautiful village," Nadine answered.

"That's not what I mean," said Peter. "I mean what kind of people would build a wall so high but not put a gate on it."

"I don't know why they didn't put a gate either," Thomas said. "But Nadine is right, it's beautiful. When you first pass where the gate should be it's like a room and a garden in one."

"What are you talking about?" Peter asked.

Thomas then said, "Okay, imagine a room six times bigger than your house. The first thing you see when you come in is a huge, gold door with God's name on it. Then you notice the opening in the roof. The roof is square. The opening is about 150 feet by 150 feet. It looks like about 75 feet on each side. If you look to the left or right you will see giant columns shaped like pyramids. The door is also shaped like a pyramid. Now back to the columns, there are only two. These must be the bottom of the two we saw with smoke coming out of them. They have a hole cut out of them at the bottom and they are burning incense in them.

"The pyramids are so majestic. It looks like they have engraved the entire Torah on them in mother-of-pearl. I can't believe that just two pyramids are holding up the whole roof. Right under the opening in the roof is a pond of fish, swans, geese, and ducks. The pond is the same size as the opening in the roof. In the middle of the pond there is a small Island. It too is beautiful. It has a palm tree. There is a peacock and a flamingo walking around. It is so beautiful."

"We are at the door now," said Paul. Paul knocked on the door of the pyramid, but no one answered.

Just then Thomas saw an alligator coming out of the water and onto the Island. He said to Peter, "There's an alligator on the island, but the other animals don't seem to be afraid of it. They are still walking around."

"God is great!" Peter shouted.

Suddenly, the door started opening. Paul called out for the others to come nearer. They all gathered at the door. The door was fully opened but no one came out or said anything. They stood there for a few minutes.

"Let's go in," Paul said. So they did. When they got inside and looked around, they saw no one. Paul said to Peter, "I don't know what's going on, there's no one here."

Peter replied, "What kind of place is this?"

"A beautiful place, we are in a synagogue," Ann said.

"I have never seen a place this beautiful," Nadine said.

"She's right," Pye said "I can't begin to describe this."

The door on the other side of the synagogue opened. A man came into the synagogue and said, "Peace be upon you."

They returned his greeting and he walked over to them and Introduced himself. "My name is Lee. I belong to the tribe of Levite."

"My name is Peter, and these are my friends." Peter introduced each person.

"What brings you all to our humble village?" Lee asked.

Peter answered. "We are looking for the man called Jesus."

Thomas then spoke up and addressed Lee. "You have a beautiful village here, but it's a little strange."

Lee smiled and said, "What is it about our village that you find strange?"

Thomas answered, "The first thing is you have a wall all around your village but no gate. Then the strangest thing happened. The synagogue door opened but there was no one on the other side of the door."

Lee laughed and said, "We have ghosts." He laughed even harder and said to Thomas, "You should see the look on your face. I was only having fun with you, my brother. The first thing you found was no gate. There is a gate at the walls. You see there are two walls close together and the gate is in between the two. Now the door, do you see that small door next to the one you came in? We have three donkeys tied to a wheel and the wheel has a rope on it that is connected to the door. We have trained them to walk around on command."

"You're being funny," Thomas said. "We don't know any command."

"You must," Lee said.

"No, we don't," Thomas answered.

Then Lee turned to the door, and told Thomas to look also. He shouted, "God is great!" and the door started to close. "Now, back to you Peter. I know of this man. A true man of God, but he has not come here. You brothers and sisters must be hungry and tired. Come with me."

"Yes, we are," Peter replied. "But we must pray first." So Peter and the others prayed. They bowed down with their faces touching the ground. They did this twice.

"Who taught you to pray like that?" Lee asked.

"This is the way all of the prophets prayed when they were in trouble," Peter said.

"I didn't know that," Lee said. "Come, let's get something to eat.

They walked through the door at the entrance of the village that Lee had come through.

Thomas said, "This is also strange."

"Not really," Lee replied. "We are the children of the God of Abraham. He is our Father. This village is set up like a house where in the best house you must first pass the father's room to get to the rooms of the children. We don't consider this village belonging to us. Everything in the heavens and the earth belongs to God. Do you understand now, my brother?"

"I understand," Thomas said.

Lee took them to a house and told them it was their house for as long as they wanted to stay. Paul and the others looked at each other and Thomas said, "This is one of the biggest houses in the village."

"Yes, it is," Lee replied. "We have two more just like this one for visitors. This house and the other two were the first houses we built. We want God's visitors to feel welcome. My wife will bring you some food. I must go tell the others we have guests."

"Thank you very much," Peter and the others said.

Lee left and Thomas told Peter, "I wish you could see this house."

"We walked down some steps," Peter said.

"Oh yeah," Thomas said. "I didn't describe the village to you. When you first come out of the synagogue, you're looking down on the village. The village is in a valley and it's shaped like a pyramid also. The house we're in is the beginning of the pyramid. There are two houses as big as this one in the back of this one."

Lee's wife entered the house and greeted everyone. They returned the greeting and she introduced herself as Lee's wife. "I have prepared food for you," she said and she and several other ladies began bringing food in and setting it on a huge table.

When they were finally done spreading all the food, Lee's wife said, "You will find everything you need to eat with in the kitchen." She pointed to the direction of the kitchen. "I must go now. If you need anything, our house is behind the other two big houses. You can't miss it. If you look between the two houses you will see it." Once again, they thanked her and she left.

"Look at all of this food," Thomas said as they all sat down together and ate.

When they finished eating they returned to the synagogue to pray. By this time men and women from the village were coming into the synagogue, also.

Lee greeted them and then he walked up to the front of the synagogue and opened up the Torah.

Thomas leaned over to Peter and whispered, "I think Lee is the rabbi here."

"Why do you say that?" Peter asked.

"Because he is standing in front of the people with the Torah opened. I believe he is getting ready to preach."

Just then Lee started to speak. "Do not follow the footsteps of the devil. Sometimes we follow the footsteps of the devil without knowing it. The devil has many people working for him. Their job is to mislead the people in any way they can. Jesus said, 'Hear and understand that it is not what goes into the mouth that defiles a man but what comes out of the mouth that defiles a man. The Pharisees were saying that Jesus was not teaching his disciples the tradition of the elders. Now, listen carefully how Jesus replied to the Pharisees, 'Why do you disobey the commandment of God with your tradition?' My brothers and sisters, don't follow the lies of the disbelievers. We know that the book that got sent down to us has been tampered with. We should know a servant of God would never change one word in His book. So, don't believe that Jesus was telling us it's okay to eat blood or the pig. Don't forget Jesus is a follower of the laws of Moses like us. We would never eat blood or the pig or tell someone it's okay to eat it and we all know that Jesus is the best of us. They are always trying to change what Jesus said, but they can never fool a true believer. Jesus has never told a lie. He tells us that there is nothing we can do without God's help. So what would make you believe that Jesus would change any of God's laws? We must ask God for help to see and hear His words only.

"All of mankind are children of God, but most of mankind do not know their father. Jesus is our brother because we have the same Heavenly Father. This is what Jesus teaches. Jesus is the way to God. I repeat, we must follow the teaching of Jesus if we want to reach God. Jesus is our brother sent to us from our Heavenly Father to bring us back home. So, do not follow the footsteps of the devil, follow the footsteps of Jesus. My brothers and sisters, I beg you, trust your heart. Your heart knows the truth. I hope I have helped someone today with my message. We have guests with us today, so greet them and make them feel at home. And if I have said anything wrong, it is from me. If I said anything right, it is from God. Peace be upon you all. Now go greet your brothers and sisters and may God have mercy on us all."

The whole congregation greeted them. Lee came over after many of the people greeted Peter, Paul, Nadine, Ann, Thomas, and Pye. "We are having dinner for you at my house, this evening," he said.

Everyone in the village came. It was a beautiful sight to see brothers and sisters laughing and telling stories about how good God had been to them. Hours passed and the stars and moon had come out to light up the night.

Suddenly, everyone started walking back towards the synagogue. Thomas turned to Lee and asked why they were all going back to the synagogue. "We pray together every night before bed. Would you like to come?" Lee said.

"Yes, I would like that very much," Thomas replied. "Peter, we are going back to the synagogue to pray again. Are you coming?"

"I guess we all are going," Peter said.

They all went and prayed. After they prayed everyone

went home.

Peter said to Thomas and Paul, "I love it here. I could stay here for the rest of my life."

"Yes, it is nice here," Thomas replied. "What do you think, Paul?"

"I think I want to go home to my wife," Paul said.

In the women's room, they were talking about the same thing. "I wouldn't mind living here because everyone is always thinking about God," said Nadine.

"You're right, they pray more than anyone I have ever seen before," Ann said. "But I don't want to stay here. I want to go back to marry Harold."

"I don't care where I live," Pye said.

"What's wrong, Pye?" Nadine asked.

"I mean, I will be happy wherever God takes me. I think I will go to sleep now."

About an hour before dawn the sound of a horn blowing woke Peter and the others up. Thomas jumped up and shouted, "We are being attacked!"

Paul ran to the window and looked out. "We are not being attacked. The horn is sounding for prayer."

"Are we going to the synagogue?" Thomas asked.

"Yes," Paul answered. They got dressed and went to the ladies' room and knocked on the door.

The women came out of the room and greeted the men. That horn terrified me at first," Nadine said.

"Just like a woman to be afraid," Thomas quickly said.

Peter and Paul started laughing. "Oh, it's funny," said Nadine.

"We are not laughing at you," Peter replied.

Let's go," said Thomas. Peter and Paul started laughing again and Paul said to Thomas, "You got us in trouble."

"Thomas is the only one of you not laughing, so leave him alone," Ann said. "Come walk back here with us, Thomas."

Thomas stopped with a smile on his face. Ann and Nadine took Thomas by his arms and they talked until they reached the synagogue. They went in and prayed. After they finished praying, they sat in the synagogue and talked about how merciful God is to mankind. They stopped talking when the sun fully came up. Then they made a short prayer and left.

They were walking back to the house when Paul said, "We should be leaving today."

They went back to the house and ate breakfast. Peter suggested they go back to the synagogue and pray for a safe journey before leaving. So, they went to the synagogue and prayed.

When they left the synagogue, Paul said, "We should go and thank Lee for being so kind." The others agreed.

They all walked together up to Lee's house. Peter said, "We're going to leave now, but we had to come and thank you for being so nice to us."

Lee replied, "Do not thank me, thank God for teaching us that all who believe in him, his messengers, and his books are brothers and sisters. You all have a home here with us and please come back to see us."

"We will. I thank God for you, my brother." Peter replied. "Peace be upon you."

"Peace be upon you, brothers and sisters. May the God of Abraham guide your footsteps."

Once they left Lee's home, Thomas asked, "Where are we going now?"

"I think we should go to Nazareth," Peter answered.

The journey to Nazareth was very quiet because they all missed Cana. They could not stop thinking about how nice the people were in Cana. Never before had any village been so kind to them. Thomas didn't even ask about eating. When they reached Nazareth, it was very late at night. They looked around for somewhere to sleep.

The next morning, they went around trying to find someone who knew something about Jesus. Everyone they asked acted like they were afraid to talk.

Thomas turned to Peter and said, "We should get out of here."

Peter replied, "We have come a long way and cannot stop looking now.

"You're right, Peter," Paul said. "Someone here will tell us something. We are going everywhere in this village until we find someone who will tell us something about Jesus."

They continued walking around asking everyone they saw. They walked up to an old man and greeted him. He returned their greeting.

"We are trying to find someone who is not afraid to talk about Jesus, son of Mary," Peter said.

"What do you want to know?" the old man replied.

They had finally found someone who would talk to them about Jesus.

The old man said, "God has blessed me with many years here on earth. No one can stop me from telling the truth. I fear only God. I will tell you everything I know about Jesus. I know him very well."

"Thank you," Peter said.

"Jesus has always been a blessing from God to all that would hear him. The Sadducees and the Pharisees have put fear in the heart of others, but not me. I will tell you about the first time I saw Jesus. It might be hard to believe but it's true. His mother came back home, she was carrying him. The people of the village saw Mary carrying a baby, and one of them said, 'O Mary, you have indeed disgraced your family. Your father was not a wicked man, nor was your mother an unchaste woman.' Mary didn't speak because she was fasting and couldn't talk to any man. So, she pointed to Jesus in her arms. The man then said to Mary, 'How can we talk to a baby in a cradle?' Then Jesus said, lying in his mother's arms, 'I am a servant of God. He has given me the Book and made me a prophet. He has made me blessed wherever I may be. He has not made me insolent. Peace be on me the day I was born and the day I die, and the day I am raised to life.' I heard that with my own ears. It's hard to believe, right?"

Peter smiled and said, "No, it's not hard for me to believe. God can do anything He wants to do. That's what makes Him God."

The old man said, "Jesus is telling us we should go back to the way we were."

Peter asked, "What way is that?"

The old man answered, "We must once again make God our King and Lord. That will be best for us if we only knew. You see, long ago God was our King and Lord until one day the elders of Israel went to the prophet, Samuel, and said, 'We want a king like all the other nations.' Samuel didn't want to tell God that but he did. Samuel also told God Israel had rejected him. God said to Samuel, 'They have not rejected you, they have rejected me.' From that day until now, we have not asked God to be our everything. The Sadducees and the Pharisees are the same people who asked for a man king. Now Jesus is telling us we must

151

ask God with all your heart to be our King and Lord again. We are in big trouble today because we don't have a king or an army to fight for us.

"We must be very careful what we ask God for because He may give it to us. That's why I pray only for God's will to be done and every day I thank him for everything he has given me and everything he will give me. I also thank him for everything he has kept from me and everything he will keep from me. I don't know where Jesus is, but may God help you find him."

"Thank you for talking to us," said Peter. "I heard everything you say and I will never forget it. Peace be upon you."

"Peace be upon you all, and may the God of Abraham be with you all," the old man replied.

They walked away and talked among themselves about where they should go next. Peter said, "Let's pray and ask God for his help. The others agreed and Peter led them in prayer.

Just then a woman came up to them crying. Paul asked her what was wrong. She told them Roman soldiers had taken Jesus away.

"Where did they take him?" Peter asked.

"I do not know," she cried.

With tears running down Peter's face, he said, "Let's go."

No one said anything, they just started walking. They walked night and day and only stopped to sleep for about an hour a night. By the time they reached the place where Jesus was they were told that Jesus was dead.

When Peter heard that Jesus was dead he fell down crying with his face on the ground. He cried and prayed all night. The others were crying also. Right before daybreak,

Peter led them in prayer. After they finished praying, the women made food.

They were eating when Peter shouted, "God is great."

"Yes, he is," the others said.

Then Peter said, "I thank God for Jesus. Jesus has changed my life. We didn't get to meet him, but I met him. Jesus took us on a journey that we will never forget. He is not dead; he lives in my heart. I will never forget what Jesus has done for me. He is our hope. We must find out all we can about him and try our best to be like him. I love Jesus, our gift from God. We should thank God every minute of the day and night for Jesus. There has never been a man like him on this earth and there will never be another. I thank you my Lord, my King, my God for blessing us with Jesus. Jesus is the only way to God. All praise is due to the creator of the heavens and the earth. I also must thank God for you brothers and you sisters. I don't have the words to say how much you mean to me. I could never thank you enough for helping me find Jesus. I hope you have found him, too. Once again, I thank you from the bottom of my heart and I love you all. I think I will go back to Cana to live. I know this is goodbye for us."

"I will go back to Cana with you before I go back home," Paul said.

"We are all going back to Cana," they said. So they left and headed back to Cana.

Hours later, they made camp so that they could rest and eat. By the time they finished eating it was almost time for the sun to set.

Peter asked Nadine to take a walk with him. She agreed with a smile on her face. They walked until they came to a hill.

"This is a nice spot," Nadine said. So, they stopped and sat down.

Only a few minutes passed when Peter asked, "Can you leave me here for a few minutes and come back to get me?"

"Okay, no problem," Nadine replied and she left.

Peter fell down with his face on the ground and started to pray. "You are my Lord, my King, and my God. If I am not Your servant I am nothing. Oh my Lord, I thank you for everything you have given me, and everything you *will* give me. I thank you for everything you have kept from me and everything you *will* keep from me. You are the all-knowing, the Wise One, and you know what's best for me. I have complete trust in you and you alone."

Peter then lifted his head from the ground and saw the sun setting. He shouted as loud as he could, "God is great. I can see!"

Nadine heard Peter shouting and started running to him. She couldn't understand why he was shouting. When she reached him he was still on his knees. Nadine fell to her knees with her arms around Peter and said, "It's okay, my love."

Peter turned to her and said, "That's a beautiful green dress you have on.

Tears ran down Nadine's face and she said, "Praise be to God!"

# The End

When you have faith in the Creator of the Heavens and the earth, and Him alone, anything is possible. "God is great!